Written by
Dani Camarena

Illustrated by
Robin DeWitt
&
Patricia DeWitt-Grush

Text copyright © 2023 by Dani Camarena
Cover Illustrations Copyright © 2023 by Robin Dewitt and Patricia Dewitt-Grush
Interior Illustrations Copyright © 2023 by Robin Dewitt and Patricia Dewitt-Grush

Published by Lawley Publishing,
a division of Lawley Enterprises LLC.
All rights reserved.

No part of this publication may be reproduced, or stored in a retrieval system, or transmitted in any form or by any means, electronic, mechanical, photocopying, recording, or otherwise, without written permission of the publisher.

For information regarding permissions, write to:
    Lawley Publishing
    Attention: Permissions Department
    70 S Val Vista Drive #A3 #188
    Gilbert, AZ 85296
    www.LawleyPublishing.com

This book is a work of fiction. Any reference to historical events, real people, or real locales are used as fiction in the work. Other names, characters, places and incidents are all a product of the author's imagination and any resemblance to actual events, locales or people, living or dead is purely coincidental.

Hardcover ISBN 978-1-958302-17-0
Paperback ISBN 978-1-958302-19-4
Library of Congress Number: 2022940950

For Nicholas and Lucas, my greatest adventure.—DC

Taken	1
Time	15
Puzzled	25
Tachyons	33
Street Gang	45
Boxcar Home	55
Luna	65
Bizarre	73
Skull	85
Q-tip Legs	93
A Daughter	103
Reunited	111
Galaxy	121

Who Knows	129
Toboggan Run	141
Mr. Automaton	151
Blimpy Ride	165
Boss	173
Whirly-Cycle	181
Metal Beast	193
Forgiveness	203
Assassin Bugs	213
Wormhole Ready	221
Secrets Revealed	235
Truth	243

1 Taken

LIGHTNING CRACKLED OUTSIDE my second-story window. The static electricity surrounded our house and forced my bangs to rise like a prickly cactus.

"*¿En serio?* Not now, Whiz." I'd named the thunderstorm after the fourth day it hovered above us. "It's been a week. You need to calm it."

I pulled my aviator goggles down over my eyes and focused on my lockbox puzzle. The box rested on my desk among a spread of sticky notes with quotes from my favorite science-fiction authors, Madeleine L'Engle and Jules Verne. Steady-handed, I branded my name into the bottom corner of the lid with a wood-burning tool. Smoky cedar wafted up to my nose with each letter carved. I-S-S-Y. A bit crooked, but it worked. I unplugged the iron and carefully placed the hot tip on a stone.

The storm rumbled and brought another explosive flash

of light. My arm hairs rose and waved like a sound rippling through water, then relaxed back against my skin. I pushed my bedroom curtain aside in time to catch a lightning bolt strike near what was left of the scorched mail post just down the muddy lane. *ZZPPT!*

I jumped back at the detonation, as did a desert spiny lizard that skittered into a hole to avoid flying splinters. Another stenciled letter from our address at 77 Yucca Road peeled off the charred metal mailbox.

What did Whiz have against letters and packages? Mathematically speaking, it was rare for lightning to strike the same spot four times within two weeks. The topsy-turvy weather whirled around our ten-acre property, yet blue skies blanketed the rest of town five miles away. Unpredictable Whiz flung charged bolts around our land day and night. I finally stopped hiding under the kitchen table a week ago.

What was it about this house?

I returned to my gadget lockbox—tweaked a gear here, twisted a screw there—when lightning shattered again. "Ow!" I flinched back and blew on my palm. The metal gears on the lid pulsed red. "What the atom?" I shoved up my goggles and threw a fist at Whiz. "You better not have fried my invention."

I poked the metal parts with my fingertip, confirming they were cool. An electrical surge could've toasted my mechanics. *Nada bueno* toward a chance to prove to Mom and Dad that I was worthy of a space in their lab. A place to perfect my gadget-making.

The lockbox mechanisms appeared undamaged by the energy shot, but I needed to check the prize secured inside. I prepared to toggle a series of small levers embedded in the lid above four painted medallions—a puzzle to solve. I flicked the levers in the order that corresponded to each medallion's picture: flower, sun, maple leaf, and snowflake. *Brilliant!* A thief would need to be extra clever to figure starting with spring. My grin could've split my face.

Three connected gears beneath the medallions began to rotate, and a tiny paddle thwacked a penny along a flat track on the lid's surface. The penny shot into a slot at the edge, releasing the latch and flinging open the top.

I lifted out my book and inspected all sides. No burn marks. Nice try, Whiz. I cuddled the book to my chest and tipped my head back, eyes closed. *My masterpiece.* It was my first completed novel. I'd even made the book cover from Aunt Maria's old leather poncho.

Mom and Dad were certain to love my book. Now, I was an

author. A scientist-author, like Albert Einstein. I ignored Mom's nagging in my head. She might disagree about my story being steampunk, but it's the best genre to fit the gadgets I imagined. I'd prove it. And my facts would show them I knew a lot about science.

Hopefully.

I set down my book and patted my cheeks to stop the frown tugging at my face—no need for that. Go time!

Trailing my hand across the desk, I grabbed my lucky number rings, a gift from Dad when I was five. They didn't quite fit anymore, but I'd never stopped wearing them. Mom insisted they protected me. I don't remember what they're supposed to save me from, but I always believed.

I slipped the thin, smooth titanium bands snugly above the knuckles of my left hand—one on my thumb, pointer finger, middle finger, and ring finger. I called them "number rings" because there are four, and four is my favorite number. It was the only integer spelled with the same number of letters as itself. Last year, Dad helped me color anodize the rings to pink, blue, gold, and purple using 9-volt batteries, baking soda, distilled water, and a stainless-steel fork.

Clink, clink. The rings were like mini finger tambourines when I tinged them together.

A quick pull of my knee-socks, one yellow, one red, and I smushed my nose against the warm windowpane. Whiz pushed an army of clouds over our yard. Little dirt bombs exploded from huge raindrops striking the path between the house and barn. *Mamá* and *Papá* were nowhere in sight. Figured. They were still holed-up in their backyard-barn-turned-science-lab.

My insides twisted. They'd promised to be back inside the house by now to hear me read my novel. Whiz must've had them up to their safety glasses with data.

I kicked my stuffed robot into a pile of wire scraps. Seriously, how much more could a girl take? I'd barely complained when they moved us from Cambridge to set up a lab in Arizona. And this June heat? 110 degrees. They must've been exposed to some loopity-loop chemical to choose this place.

Thunder rattled my bedroom window, and the pane's faded frame moaned in irritation. I pressed my forehead to the glass again. "Hello, still-empty path, void of Hector and Gina Garcia, physicists at large." I shoved off and sat on my bed.

My toes curled inside my sneakers. They'd almost missed my twelfth birthday dinner last week. All I asked of my parents was one night to share my story.

I tapped the end of a screwdriver against my forehead. What to do? Oh, yes! My hey-get-into-the-house alarm would do the trick—the one I'd made as a prototype. After my parents stayed out in their lab all night last night, not answering their cell phones, I wasn't taking any chance of getting ahold of them on my special evening.

This had been one of my most dangerous inventions. First, I'd tied a fishing line to my bedpost, strung it through my window, and crawled across the branches of our honey mesquite tree. Then, I wrapped the cord around a thick batch of leaves above the barn door and dangled chipped glass beakers from its end. On the way back to my window, I'd slipped and lost my oversized boot. It was many seconds before it thudded onto the car's hood. Glad it hadn't been me.

Well, time to put my gadget into motion. I slid the window open an inch to a wave of warm rain sprinkles, then strummed the line hard. A clattering raucous mixed with Whiz's crackled lightning sounded from above the barn. That should grab their attention. I held my breath, waiting, waiting. The pathway remained empty. My alarm needed to be louder.

Determination flooded my brain cells. Ah, scissors.

SNIP!

The fishing line jetted out the window, and a choir of shattered glass tore into the yard. Mom and Dad flung open the barn door and stopped short of the broken glass. Mom glanced toward my window with a shake of her head, then raced toward the house with Dad.

Mission accomplished.

With a hurried hand, I smoothed down my hair to nestle around my shoulders and tweaked my goggles above my forehead. I zipped from my room with book in hand and pounded down the stairs for my debut. Whiz pelted rain against the skylight in applause for my anticipated show, and lightning flashed like paparazzi cameras. I dove onto the couch two seconds before my parents burst through the front door.

Mom flung aside her coat. "Isadora! What happened? There's glass everywhere outside." She pushed her wet bangs from her eyes.

"Sorry, it was the only way I could get your attention, *Mamá*." I stood and waved my book. "Tonight's the night. Remember?"

Dad brushed raindrops from his white sleeves. "Oh, Issy, *lo siento*," he said. "We forgot. I'll make it up to you with a game of disc golf." He grinned his "forgive me" collie-dog face, then pushed up his glasses.

Disc golf. A game with me that Dad managed to find time for.

Mom eyed me. "You'll need to clean up those broken bottles, Isadora. Next time, get our attention without shattering glass all over the ground."

I was about to tell her there didn't seem to be another way, but thunder roared above. *Oh, Whiz, stop it.*

Mom stiffened and peered at the ceiling.

Lightning flashed across the backyard. She rushed to the window with Dad on her heels.

"No, you don't," I said. "The climate can wait."

Mom's shoulders jolted, and she turned to Dad. "But, Hector."

"*Papá.*" I crossed my arms, and his face relaxed, looking from Mom to me.

He guided her back to the couch. "*Está bien,* Gina."

"Okay," Mom said, but her grimace lingered. She grabbed my hand on her way to sit and pressed her fingers along each of my number rings. "*Bien,* you have on all four." She settled into the cushions. "*Querida,* did you invite anyone else to hear your story?" Her brows rose in a hopeful rainbow shape, and she toyed with her necklace, a purple cat's eye marble the size of a jawbreaker candy.

I tapped my foot and huffed. "We barely moved here to Corny-ville, *Mamá.*"

Her eyes stayed steady on mine like an unbroken electrical circuit. "Friends are important, Isadora. You need someone you can count on." She twirled the chain around her finger. "I'm sure there are kids here in *Cornville* who like science. You'll find your tribe, *querida.*"

Ugh, like I found my tribe back in Massachusetts? Not. I was too different. Kids didn't want to hang with the science geek unless they used me for projects.

She droned on, "If you'd come out of your room."

Dad gently squeezed her arm and tilted his head down, causing his glasses to slide.

She shrugged in defeat and swiped her fingers over her mouth, lips zipped.

I grinned a silent thanks to Dad and positioned my goggles over my eyes. Mom wrinkled her nose at me.

"What, *Mamá?* I need to get into character." In my best announcer's voice, I began. "Tonight's read of *The Mysterious Tales of Jocko Jones* is by none other than the author herself."

Dad clapped, and I took a bow. "Our setting is October 1886 in steampunk New York City."

Mom narrowed her eyes. "A fake world? Why not write about mathematics—"

I cut her off before she could give the "but you're my little math genius" speech. "*Mamá*, it's a *novel*." I sighed, then, back to my announcer's voice, continued, "Steampunk: an imaginary historical era, before the discovery of electricity, with machines powered by gears, pulleys, chains, and steam."

"Steam engines. *Bueno*," Dad said. He nudged Mom's shoulder with his own. "Maybe she *should* join us in the lab."

My eyes shot up, but Mom gave a curt head shake. I dropped my chin.

Nope. No way. She didn't want me in her precious space, messing it up with my gadgets. I pressed down the frustration. I still had a chance to win her over.

I waggled my novel over my head. "I'd rather write anyway." Words were *real*. "Okay, where were we?" I thumbed to the first page and turned it around for them to see. I'd pasted a black and white picture of a docked steamship with a photoshopped banner on its side that read: *Celebrate the Dedication of the Statue of Liberty, October 28, 1886.* "Jocko's investigation begins on the boat."

"Nice picture." Dad smiled.

Light zipped past the patio slider. Mom and Dad's eyes flicked to the windows behind me and the rain pouring over the roof gutters.

I waved my book. "Right here."

They returned their wide-eyed gazes to me, stiff-necked. I opened my mouth to speak again when a shimmery spot appeared above their heads. My mouth snapped shut while my eyes hypnotically focused on it, and I swayed with sudden nausea rumbling my tummy. What was it? I blinked fast, and the fuzziness disappeared.

"You okay, Issy?" Dad said.

"Yeah." *Oye*, enchilada. I shook my head, tasting my dinner in my throat. "I'm good." Mom reached for me. "*Mamá*, I'm okay," I blurted. Maybe I was dehydrated. "I'll begin again." I pushed the goggles tight to my face and raised my voice. "With eighth grade off to a start, Jocko—"

SMASH!

We all jumped at the wind slamming a patio chair against the outside family room wall. A gale blast howled about the mesquite tree, and the roof shingles clattered in an orchestra of chaos. Whiz had never been this bad before.

Mom's eyes were huge. "Hector!"

Dad heaved her from the couch. "Get down!" He stretched over the coffee table to grab my arm, but a charged blue light streaked above us and struck the wall.

"Dad!" Sparks lit around me, and a loud bang shook the house. I dove underneath the table, my heart thundering.

One Massachusetts, two Massachusetts, three Massachusetts. I counted the way Dad taught me if I were ever afraid. I squeezed my book to my chest and tightened myself into a ball. All sound slowed except a soft rain pattering on the roof.

Was it over? I crawled out into a strange wispy fog and shoved the goggles above my brows. A rotten egg scent tingled my nose.

My eyes adjusted with the fading mist, then locked onto the spotless furniture. I stiffened, dropping my book. How was the room untouched? No damage.

"*Mamá, Papá!*" Where were they? I rushed around to the back of the couch, but they weren't there. Queasiness slithered in my stomach.

"Isadora!" A faint call reached my ears. I froze.

"Mom?" My sight darted to every corner of the room, but I couldn't find her anywhere.

My chest heaved, sending me on the verge of hyperventilation. I stumbled into the kitchen, the laundry room, and the dining room. "*Papá, Mamá!*"

Empty.

I dashed upstairs two steps at a time and checked my room, the closets, the bathrooms, their bedroom. "It's going to be okay. It's going to be okay. It'll be okay." I willed the dread tightening around my ribs to release its grip on me.

"*Papá?*" The word squeaked from my raw voice. "*Mamá?*" I sunk to the floor and curled my arms over my head. Where had they gone?

"Isadora!" Mom's muffled plea came from downstairs.

I bolted up to my knees, my heart pounding, ears straining to hear the faint voice.

"We're here!"

Down the stairs, I jumped three to four steps.

"Please, Isadora!"

Where was it coming from? It was like the voice drifted up from the floorboards by the coffee table. Were they trapped underneath? I threw myself down flat and pressed my ear to the wood.

"Isadora, help!"

My eyes rounded. The voice hadn't come from below but from an object directly in front of my nose. My book!

I tore open the cover, and the voice bellowed from the pages, "Help us!"

Total tamales! "*Mamá?*"

The top sheet fluttered. I turned to the page with the steamship.

¡Oh! Mini versions of Mom and Dad stood on the dock. Mom slapped her palms against an invisible barrier. The light of an almost full moon illuminated her tormented face.

I screamed and dropped the book, scurrying backward. What had I just seen? Things like that weren't possible. Whiz must've made me loopy—I had to have imagined seeing my parents.

I leaned forward and gasped into my knees until Mom's voice pulled me out of it.

"Isadora!"

With bulging eyes, I slowly crawled to the book again, then slid open the page.

My parents jumped up and down and waved their arms on the dock. Dad yelled my name.

"How?" I whispered. Then my voice became louder. "No, no! How, *Mamá?* What happened?"

My spine gave way and slumped me against the couch. "No, no. This isn't real." I pulled the book into my lap with shaking hands and tried to study the scene.

"*Papá!*" I banged my fist on the page. My parents jumped at the thunder in their night sky, and the paper shuddered. Had I caused that?

"I'm up here. Look at me!" I gripped the book tighter.

Mom didn't respond. She sank to the wooden planks, with Dad reaching to console her as he gazed into nothingness. "Issy, if you can hear me, go to the b—"

Marching bootsteps pounded over the dock and muffled his instructions.

I leaned over the page and yelled, "*Papá*, what? What was the last part?"

Soldiers in double-breasted, red uniform jackets rushed up behind Dad. They cuffed him with metal shackles, wrenched up Mom, and dragged them away.

"No!" Where had the soldier characters come from? I hadn't written them into the plot. I flipped through the story, desperate to find any sign of movement. I got to the last page. Nothing.

My eyes froze onto the page, zoning out and brimming with tears. This couldn't be real. Could it?

Eventually, reality blazed through me. I closed the book and hugged it, desperate for a hug back. Instead, it sat cold and hard in my arms. And I knew. Mom and Dad were gone.

White light dotted my vision, and I inhaled in short bursts. Then, my mind went black.

2 Time

I WOKE THE following morning, curled in the same spot from the night before, my book snug against my chest, goggles tangled in my hair. I remembered the uncontrollable sobbing that had exhausted me into slumber. Then the nightmares began—awful images of where the soldiers held my parents and what they could be doing to them. I wakened more times than my eyes shut to sleep.

I stretched and glanced around, hoping last night hadn't really happened. But the empty house told me the truth. My dry, sticky tongue stuck to the roof of my mouth. I swallowed hard and dragged myself to the couch with a stare into emptiness. I clicked my number rings together until my ears rang. These were supposed to be my lucky rings. *Wear them all the time,* Mom had insisted. They weren't lucky at all.

But maybe? Maybe our cell phones would connect? I pulled

mine from my pocket and called Dad. The connection failed. I tried again. Failed. I dialed Mom. Same. I dialed over and over, faster and faster, hoping a signal would catch their phones, wherever they were. By the final attempt, I was inhaling so hard I'd broken out in a sweat. Chills set in. I grabbed a blanket from the couch and dragged it around me.

I dialed the local police department but hung up before it rang. No way they'd believe my parents got stuck inside a book. They'd take me away when they couldn't find Mom and Dad.

Aunt Maria would know what to do. She was my only living relative and Dad's smidge older sister. She lived near the Black Rock, New Mexico border. Not too far from us. I dialed, but it went straight to voicemail. I called back four times. I left a message on the last try, my voice desperate, "Aunt Maria, call me, bye," then tossed aside the phone.

My brain went fuzzy, and I sat in mind-numbing silence. I'd no idea how long I sat in a trance, mumbling to myself and staring at one spot.

I gazed at my book, willing my parents to pop out from the pages. Maybe if I changed the hook or the plot of my story, they'd reappear? I grabbed my laptop from the coffee table and tapped on the keyboard: "It was a dark and stormy night."

"Ugh, cliché." But it had been a dark and stormy night. I side-eyed out the window to scowl at Whiz for being such a problem, but blue sky had replaced last night's mess. I gasped, and my eyes sprung open wide—there hadn't been perfect weather over my house in what seemed like forever. Even the storm wasn't there for me anymore. I grumbled, "Thanks, Whiz, for leaving me, too."

I slammed my laptop shut then sucked in air, waiting for Mom's lecture. But I remembered I was alone, and my lower lip trembled. For once, I'd welcome her famous speech. *Isadora, don't abuse your laptop. We paid good money, and remember, honor and money are earned slowly but lost quickly.* A lump lodged in my throat. I had to get Mom and Dad back.

I opened the laptop once more and placed my fingers firm over the home keys. The blank document glared at me, a challenge to write a new scene—one that rescued my parents. Thoughts raced around my gray matter, but I couldn't slow them to make any sense.

"It won't work." I buried my face in my arms. How would I do this alone?

My breathing sped up. Stress. More oxygen would help calm me. I inhaled.

What would Jocko Jones from my story do? He always had great ideas and a great signature line: *Mighty skyscraper!* Clues. He'd gather clues.

My parents studied the weather, and the storm had whipped up worse than usual last night. Okay, first clue. I typed it out on the page. Next, a light zapped them into my book, which might be a stretch, but it was my only working hypothesis. My fingers flew over the keyboard. And then Dad told me to go somewhere that started with a *b*.

Doubt it was the bathroom. Bedroom? I already looked there. Barn? It's the only place left that starts with *b*. I set the laptop next to my book and lugged myself out the front door toward the barn. This was *not* how I wanted to win my way into their space.

The backyard lab's splintered door sat silent like two scientists had never been through it. I kicked aside the broken glass to clear the pathway, my back already sweating from the June heat. My throat tightened. If I hadn't snipped that fishing line, then my parents would've never come out of the barn and into the house. They wouldn't have gotten stuck in my book.

I shoved open the slider door, welcoming the burst of air conditioning, and my eyes flew open. "Woah, get a load of their setup."

Machines and science-y stuff cluttered the space. Brass lamps emitted a dull glow above several rows of stainless-steel tables. I flicked a glass beaker connected to a string of test tubes filled with iridescent liquid. Equipment littered the metal surfaces like a mini futuristic city, and beeping sounds came from several small machines. My stomach squirmed. Why would they keep me away from all this cool stuff?

Notes were scattered on the tables—odd sketches of stars and dark holes, next to a *Time Machine* book by H.G. Wells. Odd. It was a book from my bedroom. Why was it here? My parents weren't into science fiction. It was never factually accurate enough for them. A sidewall held a transparent wipe board with countless equations scribbled in fluorescent yellow—all in Mom's handwriting.

I searched for patterns inside the numbers. Anything to give a clue about what they learned. The complicated formulas seemed more about time measured in days and years instead of about storms. Time, like in my H.G. Wells book. My skin tingled. These numbers weren't about the weather. I reviewed the symbols in the equations over and over. The little t and big

V reminded me of a lesson I watched online. I recalled that *t* was for dilated time, and *V* meant velocity. A cold numbness spread across my forehead. Time travel?

My brain cells fired off. I stumbled over to a ratty couch and flopped down on the cushions. Time travel. For real? No, impossible. I mulled over the clues for almost an hour when a shout came from outside the barn entrance.

"Issy, you there?" The heavy Spanish accent lit my spirit, and I raced to the door.

"*Holá*, Issy. There you are." Aunt Maria greeted me at the entrance and eyed a piece of glass I'd missed. She fanned herself with her hand, sending the silver bracelets stacked up her wrist clattering in a frenzy. "Everything okay?"

"*Tía!*" I barreled forward and locked my arms around her waist. Tears brimmed my eyes. I wasn't alone. "I called and called, but you didn't answer."

"*Oye*, I'm happy to see you, too." She laughed. "You know me and that complicated cell phone. We're no *amigos*." She stroked my hair, then squeezed out of my grasp. "It's *caliente*." She bustled in and shrugged up her oversized turquoise purse to her shoulder. Her brownish-red hair waved wild around her face. "I was on my way back from a road trip to Vegas, for you know, bingo." She winked. "I stopped for gas and heard your voicemail. I was pretty close. Thought I'd come straight here to see if everything's okay—you sounded *no bueno. Ahora, dónde está mi hermano?* I'm sure my brother is up to something."

"Um." How would I explain? Who would believe it? I wasn't sure I did.

"Come, *mija*. Where are your parents?" She fiddled with

her necklace—one the same as Mom's, a cat's eye marble. Dad gave it to her as a thank you for helping us move.

"They're gone. I, I—" My words sunk with my heart.

"Hmmm." She raised one of her thick, shaped eyebrows. "Issy?"

"I'll explain at the house, *Tía*." She needed to be sitting in her favorite rocking chair for this.

We walked the short path to the front door and into the family room. Aunt Maria commented on the hot weather while she parked herself in the chair and plucked a half-knitted purple scarf from her purse. Oh boy, she could knit for hours. I sat on the couch and tried to keep myself together so that I wouldn't upset her. I failed.

"*Ahora,* Issy, why did you call and call—" She gasped at the sight of my glossy eyes and heaved herself over beside me, drawing me in. "*Mija,* what has happened?"

My words broke like a thunderstorm. "I read my story to them. But then the rain came stronger. Wind, too." I waved my arms and hoped she followed my thoughts. "The roof shook, lightning inside the house, Mom and Dad, they were gone." My last words choked out, "Th-they disappeared. Inside my book."

For some reason, Aunt Maria didn't ask any questions. She didn't seem confused, either. She sucked in a breath and made the sign of the cross. Seconds passed before she let the air leak out. "Now, now, *mija.*" She plucked a magazine from the coffee table and waved it across her face. She whispered up to the ceiling, "*Sí,* I knew something bad would happen."

I snapped up my chin and pushed away from her. "You knew what?"

"*Aye-yai-yai*," she said and settled into the couch pillows. "Where to begin?"

"How about *Mamá*, *Papá*, and time travel?"

Her hand flew to her chest. "You know?"

Everyone knew, except me. "Had an idea from what's in the barn, and now you've confirmed it."

"*Sí.* Tricky, Issy."

No. My parents tricked me. They lied about their weather research. No wonder they wouldn't allow me in their lab. "When did it all start?"

She fiddled with her bracelets. "As you know, your parents were physicists at NASA."

I nodded at their award plaques on the bookshelf.

Aunt Maria flapped the magazine before her paled face. "They investigated time travel." She glanced behind her shoulder, the coast clear, and continued, "They discovered a portal—a wormhole to be exact, here in Arizona."

I shook my head. "How do you know?"

A blush crept into her cheeks. "*Chica Cotilla*, my brother calls me. Nosey sister. When I helped you all move in, I overheard them talking about it." She threw a flippant hand. "This house is small, no? Anyway, your father caught me, swore me to secrecy like we were kids, except he left out the blood oath part."

My gut gurgled. It was obvious where the wormhole was, and Mom and Dad had kept it a secret from me. "The wormhole is here in the house." I clanked my number rings. Could that be what Whiz was?

Aunt Maria's eyes fell. "I guess so, *mija*. They must've time traveled in the hole."

"Ridiculous." I grabbed my book and smacked it onto the coffee table. "They yelled at me from inside there. They went into *my* book, set in a *fake* steampunk world." My mind was fuzzed. "That's not time travel, right?"

"*Mija, Yo no sé* how time travel works or how your book got into the mix."

I clasped my hands together. It didn't matter how it happened. Mom and Dad were gone. "It's my fault. I forced them out of their lab to listen to my story."

"You didn't do this," Aunt Maria said. She raised her eyes, muttered a prayer, and made the sign of the cross again. "Your parents knew the risk."

Tears flooded my vision. "What kind of parents would risk leaving their daughter?"

Aunt Maria backpedaled. "I'm sure they didn't imagine they'd ever open the wormhole."

"Doesn't make sense." I sniffled. "Why move here if they couldn't open it?"

"*No sé.*" She settled back into the rocking chair and flung up her hands, rattling her bracelets.

"I know." A deep loss seared my soul. All those hours they spent in the lab, all the secrets—they lied about what was really going on. How could they do that? Frustration pounded my head. I stood and squared off to Aunt Maria, shouting, "They're more interested in their science than in me!" My legs buckled, sending me to the floor.

Aunt Maria lowered herself next to me and wrapped her arm around my shoulder. "You have a right to be mad. My brother, he chases his dreams. Your mom has high ambitions.

23

But above all, they love you."

"They sure show it." Not. I pulled down my goggles over my eyes and huddled into my arms.

"*Mija*. Do not hide your feelings." Aunt Maria pushed the goggles back up. "You're beautiful in here." She tapped my chest. "And smart here." She palmed my head. "Now, let me take you to my home."

"No." I stood. "I won't leave them. They're here somewhere, stuck in my book or . . . I don't know. Why'd they have to uproot my life for some strange interstellar thing?"

"Oh, *mija*." Aunt Maria's chin shook. "*Lo siento mucho*. They must've had a good reason."

Mom and Dad said the move was for a slower pace of life, to spend more time together. Time. How ironic. But now I saw the truth. They wanted the wormhole, not me.

Well, too bad for them. They were *my* parents, and *I* wanted them. Like Dad said last year after arguing with Aunt Maria for a month, *You never give up on family. Ever.*

I nodded to Aunt Maria. "Get ready, *Tía*. We're going after them."

3 Puzzled

COLOR INCHED BACK into Aunt Maria's face, but her forehead furrowed with deep lines.

"I don't know how to find your parents, Issy," she said. "Your dad's smarts trump mine."

"We have to try." I stood and waved her up. "There might be clues in the barn. They were working out there right before the lightning hit."

Aunt Maria rose and steadied herself, hand clutched around her necklace.

"*Tía,* are you okay?"

"*Sí, sí.*" She stepped near me. "*Mija,* your father told me if anything peculiar happened, that I should take you away from here."

I flinched. "No. I can't leave them." A sunbeam penetrated the window and heated my legs. Like on the beach with Mom, when she'd cover my feet with cozy sand. I stifled a cry. "They caused this, but who else will help them?"

Aunt Maria stuck out her bottom lip and blew a puff of air, ruffling the curls above her brows. "Okay. I'll help you. But first, you rest."

A smile dared take over my lips. It was hope. "Okay, Aunt Maria. I'll snooze." Last night's fidgety sleep of bad dreams sent me into a big yawn. I laid on the couch and snuggled into the pillows. My mind worked on a plan until the black hole of exhaustion took over.

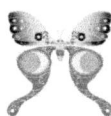

BY THE TIME I'd woken, the late afternoon sun had painted a sky of pinks and oranges above the Agua Dulce Mountains. I followed Aunt Maria, who balanced a tray of cookies out the porch door and set it onto the patio table. Warm *polvorones de canelé*—best cinnamon cookie, ever.

"Mmm, Aunt Maria," I said between chews. "It's all I ever want for meals."

"Ah, *bien*. These *polvorones* gotta be good." A hot breeze whipped around the porch, scattering napkins over the deck, followed by a smattering of raindrops. Aunt Maria tilted up her face. "Smell something?"

A sharp zing of earth and iron hit my nostrils. "Mom says that odor comes from the ozone—" I jumped at the electric bolt cracking above. Rain poured. "We'd better get to the lab."

Aunt Maria plucked an umbrella from a porch bucket. I

raced for the barn while she eased herself down the stairs. I flung open the wood door. Aunt Maria walked in a few moments behind, and her jaw unhinged.

"Pretty awesome, huh?" I eyeballed a side table that would make a perfect work spot for my experiments. I wished.

My *tía* tapped her long pink fingernail on a glass cabinet. Behind the enclosure hung two bright yellow hazmat suits. "*Mi hermano* worked on serious stuff." She poked around while I tried calculating Mom's math. Lines, numbers, and squiggles made up impossible equations.

Rain crashed against the barn's side, sending a tingle up my spine like a line of ants. *Whiz, is that you?*

"Issy, look." Aunt Maria aimed her finger at an old wardrobe mirror.

The oval antique frame was out of place amongst the tech. I peered at my reflection, and a spark pulsed from behind the glass.

A zing of static crackled across my skin and through my number rings. "Oh!" I jumped at the zap and shook out my hand. My eye caught sight of a butterfly outline flickering under the mirror's surface before it disappeared.

"Did you see that?"

Aunt Maria bustled over. "No, *mija*, what happened?"

"The mirror. It lit up from the inside." I knocked my knuckles along the mirror's back, but no more sparks. "Could have been a weird lightning reflection."

I turned to take in the whole room.

Bookshelves lined one barn wall from floor to ceiling. Maybe there was a book on how to open a wormhole. I shoved a ladder attached to the case, rolling it a few inches along the edge. The top shelf was three times higher than I was tall.

Random subjects peppered the titles at eye level. A book by Gloria Cloudless: *Weather This or That.* No titles mentioned wormholes, though. I'd have to climb high for the good ones. My arms shook. Mom once told me that bravery comes from the heart and the mind. Our mind had to help the heart overcome its emotion. *Come on, mind, do your thing.* I climbed past rows of books about jet streams, atmosphere, precipitation, but *nada* about time travel.

Near the top, my stomach flipped through itself, and I hugged the ladder. How would I find my parents without any idea of how this stuff worked? I'd have to live with Aunt—

A gentle whirring sound at my far right kicked off. "That doesn't sound right."

I grabbed the shelf's edge and pulled the ladder toward the noise—an ornate metal box. A fast click joined in with the whirs. I held my breath, ears wide open.

The riveted box, about a foot in width and height, was stowed between two thick books, their spines covered in random gold-leafed letters. A spoked wheel sat flush on the box's outer side with various gears set behind it. A large gear rotated and kicked a smaller one into motion, clicking like that wheel on Nana's favorite game show, *Wheel of Fortune.*

I pulled on the box, but it wouldn't budge. Something was way off about it. Its industrial look didn't match Mom's homey taste in decorations. Plus, it was so high up in the bookcase. *Nada* easy to reach.

The two books on either side had no titles. On closer examination, they weren't books at all. Just painted wood. I

tapped each to the tune of a hollow *thunk*. With a tug on one, it tilted and clicked to a stop. A panel in the back of the bookcase behind the chest slid open. My hand shook with excitement, and I repeated the motion with the other book. Tilt. Click. The metal box vibrated and slid backward through the open panel.

No! I stretched my fingers to grab it before—

"*Tía*—" I startled. The box dropped into an unseen space behind the bookcase. It scraped along the barn wall on its descent, dust flying from each shelf it passed. I followed the sound with my eyes, and the box crash-landed, shocking Aunt Maria to jump right out of her skirt.

"Oh my!" She yanked it up over her leggings, then dissolved into frantic fanning with a *Physics World* magazine.

"Sorry!" I scuttled down the ladder, dropped the last few feet, and scrambled on my knees to the bottom shelf, where a click-click sounded from behind the lower books. I flung aside a few and found a small hatch door on the bookcase wall. It cranked open on its own. A platform pushed the ornate metal box forward and deposited it on the floor with a thud.

The platform shot backward, slamming the hatch shut.

"*Aye-yai-yai.*" Aunt Maria bent over and rapped the metal container with her knuckles while I plopped cross-legged on the ground, facing the spoked wheel side.

Rivets and bronze screws decorated the top lid. Its design was way more advanced than the stuff I made. "Aunt Maria, you know what this is?"

"*No sé,*" she whispered.

"A puzzle box."

"Oh, like a trick box to hide things in, no?"

"Yes, a secret compartment." Scooching around to the next side, I found four square buttons with etched pictures. The top left displayed a cocoon, the top right a caterpillar, the bottom left a tree branch, and the bottom right a butterfly. A butterfly? I narrowed a peek at the nearby wardrobe mirror. Its dark glass mocked me.

"*Aquí*, maybe an opening," Aunt Maria said. She pointed to the third side.

I leaned over and poked at a pewter kaleidoscope cover. "Shut tight."

On the fourth side, three pin-sized holes formed a row in the center, surrounded by an intricate pattern of gold swirls, leaves, and grommets.

"How do we open it?" She tugged on the lid.

"We need to solve each side," I said.

I scooted back over to the four raised squares and pushed my thumb on the caterpillar. The picture pressed flush to the box's surface. "They're buttons." A quick shove on the other three images, but *nada* triggered.

"Now what?" Aunt Maria said.

"We try again." I reset the pictures with a tap on each and studied the images: cocoon, caterpillar, tree branch, butterfly. Caterpillar to a butterfly. Yes, that was it. "The lifecycle of a butterfly."

"*¿Qué?*" Aunt Maria shook her head.

"We press the pictures in the order of how a butterfly grows." I pushed in the first logical one. "Tree branch, because, well, a caterpillar attaches to a branch." In went the square with the fuzzy caterpillar next. "Then he spins himself a snuggly home."

I applied pressure to the cocoon square. "And he later comes out as a butterfly." I selected the last image, and the gears spun, triggering the clicking wheel.

"It's working." Aunt Maria bent sideways and ogled at the contraption's movement.

I hurried around to the kaleidoscope. It gyrated open, revealing a hole with a knob inside. I reached in and turned it. The cocoon image on the other side sprung open. A small brass object tinged to the floor. Aunt Maria picked up the half-circle disc, about the size of her thumb, and handed it to me. Three straight pins protruded from its flat edge.

I displayed the disc in my palm. "I know exactly where this goes."

4 Tachyons

I MOVED AROUND the box to the side with the three holes.

"Oh, Issy, *muy bien,* you got it." Aunt Maria bopped up and down with a smile.

The three pins lined up with the three holes, and the disc slid in. The wheel whirred.

My heart skittered along with the box lid edging up like a slow-motion jack-in-the-box. The top stopped upright. I stuck my head over the opening, listening to a rapid tick. A buzzy sensation rippled my skin.

"Oh!" I flung away my face.

Aunt Maria reeled backward. "Watch out!"

Up from the box rose a metal something with wings.

What the atom? A brassy insect, wings spread out the size of a softball, hovered above my head. "*Tía,* it's some sort of mechanical butterfly." I couldn't take my eyes off the intricate details. Machine, yes, but also elegant. And clever?

Rain clattered on the roof with the mounting storm outside. Whiz was back. We needed to hurry, but the butterfly held my attention.

The gear-speckled creature lowered before my face. Its copper wings, each adorned with gold wire swirled in the shape of a crescent moon, clicked and clacked to stay in one spot. It flew at my face. I ducked, but the butterfly prepared for another launch.

Aunt Maria grunted to a stand and slid off her *chanclas*. "Back up, Issy. I got this," she said.

"No, don't." I moved between her and the struggling creature. The butterfly wasn't vicious. It was scared.

"I'll protect you." Aunt Maria swung her sandal, and the butterfly dipped underneath.

"Don't hurt it!" I waved my hands in front of Aunt Maria's face.

But she focused only on the metal insect. "I got it!" Aunt Maria swatted again.

I silently cheered as the butterfly dodged the blow, but it came at me again, aiming to land on my shoulder.

Aunt Maria screamed and hocked her sandal.

I raced to her and held her back in a hug. "Stop, *Tía*, please."

"But, but . . ." Her chest heaved, and she gulped for air. The butterfly clicked and clanked with watchful lenses as Aunt Maria sat on the floor. "*Lo siento, mija.* I'm sorry. You are my responsibility while your parents are gone."

I fanned her with a magazine. "You're doing a great job, Aunt Maria. You've got this. Let the butterfly land."

She wiped her face with the hem of her skirt. "*Bueno,* Issy."

I held up my hands to the insect. "We won't hurt you," I said. The butterfly twitched its wiry antennae. "Promise, we won't." I stepped back.

It clapped its wings, fell into a drift, and settled on the box's edge.

I knelt closer, and the butterfly clacked at me. A tiny gear shot off its wing. I raised my palms. "It's okay." The mechanical insect gave its elongated body a gentle heave.

Aunt Maria leaned in. "Maybe she's tired."

I side-eyed her. "What makes you think it's a girl?"

"Her design *es muy bonita.* Tints of pink and green on her wings." The butterfly waved in response. "Look underneath. Twirls of tiny gold chain."

"Aren't ya glad you didn't whack this beautiful thing after all?" I teased.

Aunt Maria smirked. "Oh, *no sé.* Her parts would make

cool earrings."

The butterfly pointed her antennae at my *tía* like a bull, ready to charge.

"Okay, okay." I put my hand between them. This butterfly was lit. "Let's figure out how she works."

I placed my finger near the butterfly's copper wire legs. She dipped her face to my skin. Had she smelled me? "Come, jump on," I urged her.

She brought her wings together with a gentle click and stepped one jointed appendage onto my fingertip, then the other five. My skin tingled. I turned my hand, and she crawled into my palm. Her tiny feet poked me like dull pencil tips. I lifted her. No battery pack underneath. "She is amazing! And beautiful. Not sure where she could've come from."

Aunt Maria moved in close. The butterfly flicked its forewing at her nose. "Ow! That ball of paper clips attacked me."

I choked on my laughter. "She's letting you know you're in her space."

"Space? Hmph, *esa mariposa* belongs in outer space."

The butterfly turned and raised her behind. My giggle fit almost made me drop the creature.

Her odd design was nothing I'd ever seen. Aunt Maria had joked about outer space. But? I dragged my eyes up to a dead stare at my *tía*. "Do you think she is from another world?"

Aunt Maria's mouth opened in a silent *Oh*.

I turned my hand, searching for a clue on the butterfly. *CRASH!*

Lightning lit the barn window. The creature jabbed my palm with its front legs before flitting up near my head.

"What does she want?" I said. Was the butterfly reacting to Whiz?

She flew high, gliding. A glint reflected off her underbelly, and I caught sight of a small crank. I reached up for her to land on my arm, but her wings jittered. Her eye lenses widened. With a final shudder, the butterfly's wings seized, sending her to the floor with an awful crunch.

"Oh, no!" I clambered over to her on my knees to help her feel safe while Whiz pounded rain on the barn roof. Two of the butterfly's legs bent the wrong way. Her wings appeared unbroken, but a half-dozen gears lay around her.

"*Más* awful." Aunt Maria shuffled over and poked at the butterfly's body.

"You have to be okay," I told the butterfly, my voice cracking.

"*Mija*, it's okay. She wasn't alive."

"I know, but she's the link to Mom and Dad. She has to be. They went to the trouble of hiding her inside a puzzle box."

I picked her up and cradled her in my hands. "She looks mostly okay."

"What if you wind her up?" Aunt Maria said.

"Huh?"

"Like a music box." Aunt Maria pointed to the crank on the butterfly's abdomen.

"*Tía*, great idea." My emotions had clouded any logical thought. I set her on the workbench. My fingernails could barely nick the crank, but I latched on and eased it to the right. "Look!"

The butterfly's legs twitched.

"Turn it more." Aunt Maria clasped her hands.

Another full rotation. "Please be okay." She wiggled her

good legs and worked the injured ones into shape. With a flick of her wings, she pushed herself upright and turned her lenses to me. She nodded at the fallen gears.

A smile plastered across my face. Was this really happening? I was about to repair a mechanical insect in my parent's lab. This was all I ever wanted, but of course, with Mom and Dad here, working side-by-side on gadgets and experiments.

I pinched together my brows and chewed the corner of my lip. The tiny gears slipped from my grasp. Darn.

Nearby sat the tools I needed: tweezers and a magnifying glass.

The butterfly held her wings still, allowing me to locate tiny pegs for the gears. I slid one on, and she vibrated until it settled into place. I added another, pausing to allow her to quiver. After the final gear, she lifted off and settled onto the puzzle box's edge.

"*Bueno.* You fixed her, Issy."

My shoulders raised. "I did."

Aunt Maria moved to poke the butterfly, but the insect snapped her wings. "Ooh, she's feisty. Now what?"

"Not sure." I had no clue what to do with an intelligent robotic butterfly.

Before I could ponder ideas, the rain crashed harder. The butterfly rose on her hind legs, rearing like a horse, and turned her other legs inward.

"*Mariposa* is pointing at something," Aunt Maria said.

In response, the butterfly clapped her wings.

Three tiny levers stuck out from her upper chest. I gripped the first with the tweezers and pulled. A whirring came from the butterfly, no louder than a laptop fan. The second lever squealed like a teakettle whistle. The third eased into position, and the butterfly settled down on all six legs. She spread her wings. Steam rose from a ridge in the center of her back, and panels on each side slid open.

Aunt Maria stared in awe. "Something's inside."

I plucked out a small object. "A flash drive."

The butterfly snapped shut and remained still.

"Guess she has done her job." Aunt Maria shrugged.

"We shouldn't leave her out in the open. My parents hid her for a reason."

A glass jar from the lab table held the butterfly snug. I fastened the lid and wrapped the container in Mom's blue sweater from the coat rack before placing the butterfly into Dad's backpack. I slung the bag over my shoulders and grasped the flash drive.

Aunt Maria thumbed her nose. "What do we do with that little plastic thing?"

I grinned. "We see what secrets it holds."

We hustled to the house, dodging rain and ducking the thunderous roars. Whiz came in fast, threatening to crack a lightning whip. If Whiz was the wormhole, then I needed to be ready for a chance to get to my parents.

Aunt Maria and I stumbled into the house and slammed the front door shut. I ran up to my bedroom, careful not to jostle the butterfly jar. I grabbed a couple of inventions I'd made from my story and added them to the backpack. Best to be prepared. I pulled the backpack straps tight, keeping the bag snug against my back and the butterfly safe.

Downstairs, I had Aunt Maria zip my book into a side pocket

of the backpack. I sat on the floor and opened the laptop on the coffee table. It took ages to load. Aunt Maria settled onto the couch, knitting, but the yarn fell off her needles more than the number of loops she could make. The events had rattled her nerves.

"Okay, ready." I pushed the flash drive into a USB port. Auto-play pulled up several folders on the screen. "Look at this."

Aunt Maria heaved herself to the couch's edge and squinted. "Wormhole, space-time, stability, exotic matter. What in the world are in those folders?"

I clicked the wormhole folder and jumped at a lightning zap that lit the room. "One-thousand one, one-thousand two, one-thousand three . . ." I counted to ten before thunder clapped in the distance.

"Why do you count?" Aunt Maria said.

"Because the number of seconds between lightning and thunder, divided by five, is how many miles away the lightning struck."

Aunt Maria counted on her fingers. She sighed and tucked a blanket around her waist.

"Yeah, a storm's near," I said. "Like the night my parents disappeared."

I selected the one file inside the wormhole folder, and a slide show began to play. Pictures of cosmic pits appeared, each flecked with countless stars on the outskirts of *nada*-ness. Swirling masses of purple, orange, and blue light formed two holes next to each other on a flat surface.

"It says here each hole represents a point in time."

The next photo showed the flat surface folded over itself.

The holes lined up with one another—one hole above, one below, with a tunnel running between.

"A wormhole can fold time like paper, making two parts of it closer together. You can go into a wormhole from one time and travel the passage to an exit in another time."

Aunt Maria shook her head. "Science-y stuff makes me *loca*."

"Let's check the stability folder." I clicked the icon, and a single document appeared. I scanned the text then gave Aunt Maria a brief explanation. "The path between the two wormholes needs stability, or it falls in on itself. Exotic matter keeps the hole stable."

A sliver of hope warmed my insides as Whiz built up outside. I nodded at Aunt Maria. "The storm is strong. If my theory is right, the wormhole will open again, and then we use exotic matter to keep it steady." I pulled up my knee socks and wiggled my goggles down over my eyes.

"*Oye*, my brain is overloaded. Go inside a random hole? Issy, it's too much for us. Wormholes, exotic whatevers. We know *nada* about it."

I had no comeback. She was right. I didn't have experience with wormholes. My brief moment of hope shattered, and I slammed my fist on the table, giving Aunt Maria a startle. She frowned, and the crevice between her eyes deepened.

Another lightning bolt streaked outside. "One-thousand one, one-thousand two—" Thunder pounded above. "Less than half a mile away. Please, *Tía*, we have to try."

"*Pronto*, what does it say about exotic matter?"

I tried to remember anything I'd read from science books. "Physical objects are made of positive matter, like my book.

Paper is the matter. But exotic matter." I continued reading in my head because it got way more complicated. "It has negative energy." My head hurt, and Aunt Maria's attention wavered. "We need something called a tachyon to keep the wormhole open."

"A tacky what?" She gave her head a sharp waggle.

I re-read the passage. "Pronounced *tacky-on*. A particle, faster than the speed of light."

"Woah, beyond me. Maybe we should—"

Blue lightning hit the mesquite tree only twenty feet from our house, sending branches cracking apart. Whiz!

It was so close it sounded like a bomb had exploded. I screamed and jumped to my feet, jostling the butterfly jar against my back. "It's happening again. Hurry, *Tía!* Wormhole's gonna open."

Aunt Maria struggled to push herself off the couch, yelling, "What about the tacky stuff?"

"No time! We'll figure it out." I pressed my goggles tight to my face.

Was I ready for whatever I'd find on the other side? We had no guarantee of making it to Mom and Dad. My feet fumbled, trying to get me away from Whiz, but I forced my toes to hold firm. I was the only one who could find my parents. Lightning sparked again. "Aunt Maria, come on!"

She stepped back. "*Mija*, I don't think this is a good idea. Don't do this. We're not ready—"

I shouted the first sentence of my book from memory. Wind blew around us, whipping our hair. Thunder crashed. My hand shot out to her. "Grab on, *Tía!*"

Words from my story screamed from my mouth, and a blue

lightning bolt blasted from the fireplace. The light halted midair, turning into a spiraled hole, sparking purple, orange, and blue. My head ached fiercely with my churning stomach.

"Issy!" Aunt Maria lunged, and her dress caught. She tripped over the coffee table.

I stretched my arm, her fingertips mere inches away, when a blast jerked me backward. A kaleidoscope of colors sparked around me. I slammed my eyes closed, and my body went into freefall.

5 Street Gang

I FLUNG MY arms in a useless attempt to control my plunge. My hand hit against a rough object, and I landed hard on my backside with a loud thud. *Ouch!* I peeked open my eyes and rubbed my rump before pushing up my goggles.

"Wait, what?" I was sitting on the cold, hard ground underneath a metal staircase. Alone. "Oh, no!" Aunt Maria hadn't gotten to the wormhole in time. Was she okay? Hurt? My head throbbed worse than any headache I'd ever had, and the screaming seagulls above made it worse. I dug my palms into my temples to press out the pain. My ragged panting made it hard for me to catch my breath. I sucked in air until my thundering heart began to calm. Somehow the wormhole remained stable for my passage, but I'd no idea how without me having tachyons.

I peered at my surroundings. Pipes ran up the length of the wall to my side, spurting steam from vent holes dotted along its surface. Cold bit at my bare arms. I scuffled up to a crouch, but my tummy churned, throwing off my balance and sending me backward into a slime-covered wall.

"The butterfly!" My yell must have scared the grubby black rat who'd scurried over my shoe. I shrugged off my backpack and peeked inside. *Mariposa* sat unharmed in the jar, waving her wings at me. Mr. Rat came sniffing around again. I shooed him toward three wooden barrels stamped with R.H. Macy & Co., New York City. The rodent skittered behind a rag pile.

A deep inhale helped to rid my stomach of the icky feeling, and I crawled over to the underside of the stairs for a peek out between the steps. About twenty feet away, a narrow, wet cobbled sidewalk played like an old-time movie at sunset. Men, women, and children dressed in trousers, long skirts, corsets, and leather jackets walked the path.

I raised a brow at a mechanical, steam-snorting horse passing by the sidewalk. "Total tamales," I whispered. Where had I ended up?

Heavy footsteps fell above. I scuttled back a bit.

"That statue gets dedicated this month," a man said.

"Aye, it be a nice lady of bronze," a woman replied.

A worn set of boots clanked down the stairs, followed by smaller feet encased in tan leather heels. They stopped on the steps. Something familiar about their footwear drew me forward. Tiny gears and rivets adorned the strangers' shoes. I gasped. Like the costumes of my book's steampunk world. Like the gears on the mechanical butterfly. A tingling spread through my chest. How was any of this possible?

The gruff voice continued. "Not sure why the French

gave it to us."

She tsked at him, and they went on their way.

I grabbed my book from the backpack. Page one hadn't changed since the night my parents were sucked in—a grassy area, the almost full moon, a docked steamship with the Statue of Liberty's dedication banner.

My mind wobbled, unable to catch up with the facts of where I'd landed. The man had said the statue from the French would be dedicated this month. Which I hoped meant that I was at the same time as the picture in my book—when the soldiers took my parents. My heart somersaulted.

I peeped out through the stairs again, then saw it across the street, through the passing people—the grassy area, the docked ship, the fluttering banner. My story! But how? It would have to be an alternate dimension because steampunk wasn't real. Right? My breathing became ragged again. "It'll be okay," I told myself. I'd written this world, so I should know it. That would help me along.

There was no sign of my parents or a hint of the brutal storm from the night the soldiers took them. Ideas churned on how to find Mom and Dad. The air in front of me shimmered and rippled. I blinked fast, and the ripples disappeared. Traveling through time must've wiped me out.

Coldness feathered my arms with the retreating sun. I grabbed Mom's blue sweater from my backpack and slipped it over my head before snuggling into the faint scent of her lavender perfume. Rummaging the backpack pockets only gave me Dad's calculator. He still liked the old battery-powered kind. It wouldn't do me any good here.

47

A cry pushed through my lips. I was alone. And poor Aunt Maria. She was probably in agony like I was after losing Mom and Dad. Aunt Maria should be here. How could I do this by myself?

Cold air swirled the stairwell. It sent leaves twirling around my feet and me into quivering convulsions. A night outside in New York City during October would be tough to survive. And if I didn't make it, then neither would my parents. I had to push on.

First thing—figure out *when* I am in this timeline. Did I arrive before or after Mom and Dad?

I traced my finger around the moon in the picture of my book. Darkness tinged the left side, and the rest of its surface was lit up. A near-full moon. Yes! The monthly lunar phases would tell me about what time they'd arrived.

Last year's astronomy class hovered in my mind. First-quarter moon is before a full moon. As the moon moves into whole light, darkness inks the left edge—a waxing gibbous moon. I rechecked the picture in my book:

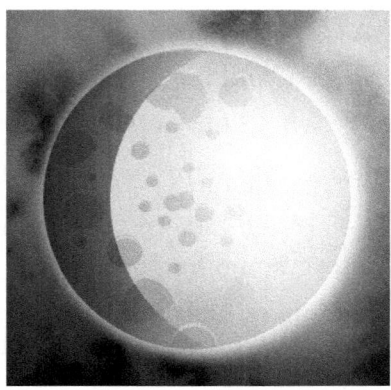

Murkiness shadowed the moon's left edge. Mom and Dad were taken into my book at the waxing gibbous moon phase, after the first-quarter moon. I slid the novel into my backpack, careful of the butterfly jar, and slinked out from the stairwell. The moon here should be in the waxing gibbous phase. Like in my book. My insides vibrated. I'd find Mom and Dad soon.

Crowds on the sidewalk had begun to dwindle, and the pavement glistened under the glow of gas lamps lighting around me. I wrapped my arms around my shoulders and tiptoed out beyond the stairs, following the wall to the corner of the brick building. I concealed myself behind a downspout.

Across the street, my eyes followed the skyline above the docked ship to the moon. No, wait! That couldn't be. I stared at the orb, my mouth turning dry. Light lit only the right half.

First-quarter moon. I'd arrived *before* my parents.

Hope sliced through my soul, leaped out, and left me far behind. First-quarter moon to a waxing gibbous took close to a week. Six nights until Mom and Dad arrived. Instead of a rescue mission from jail, I'd have to stop the soldiers from taking my parents. Impossible! I. Could. Not. Fight. Soldiers.

I huddled near the wall. My eyes burned with each question racing around my mind. What would I do in the meantime? Where would I stay? What if my parents somehow never showed up, and I got stuck in 1886?

"Think, Issy. Think." I had to act like Jocko Jones. Heck, I'd written him to be an expert on the streets. *Mighty skyscraper!* He'd find the local market, blend in, play on people's kindness for warm clothes, food, a bed.

I pushed away from the wall. A loud shout startled me, and

two guys staggered around the corner. Not characters from my story. My eyes searched fast around me for an escape route. The men blocked my path to the street, and the stairwell would corner me in.

"Aye, what we have here?" A short, round man with greasy hair stepped closer. His red-blotched face dripped with sweat. He snickered. "Getta load of her clothes."

I pulled Mom's sweater tight around my middle and slowly backed toward the stairs. My legs shook uncontrollably, almost sending me to the ground. What did these guys want?

"Interesting outfit you's got there," he said. "Can't match your sock colors?" He melted into a fit of laughter.

Greasy himself wore a dingy, long-sleeved collared shirt and brown leather vest decorated with brass gears. A handful of keys and two pocket compasses hung from his thick neck. A sort of brace made with brass rods, pistons, and copper tubing encased his arm. Maybe I could get by him, and his arm wouldn't be fast enough to grab me with all that gear weighing it down.

Before I could think, Greasy lunged at my backpack. I sidestepped, sending him into a faceplant on the wall. "Ow! Why'd you's do that?"

The second guy towered over six feet tall. He pushed his hand through his crew cut and flicked his eyes between my backpack and a smartphone-sized metal contraption hanging from his belt. He furrowed his brow at me before pulling Greasy from the wall. "Fool, Chunk. Always desperate to make a pal, you snucker."

I gritted my teeth, stamping down my panic. I needed to run. Chunk howled, "Aw, come on, Sal. I could use a new buddy."

He wobbled forward with a belch of vomit breath, and I slapped away his hand.

My heart hammered. There was no way I could fight off two thieves. I considered a scream but choked on my spit. A humming sound caught Sal's attention, and he snatched up the little box from his waist. His narrowed eyes followed the gear movements; then, he set his focus on me.

I held up my hand, palm out. "Hey, I don't want trouble." Moonlight glinted off my number rings.

The gears on the little box halted, and Sal smacked it against his thigh. "Piece of junk." He grabbed my wrist and twisted me into his side.

"Let me go!" Fear sliced my chest, and I couldn't inhale. I struggled against his hold.

Sal pushed his brass eyeglasses up to his forehead. Lenses and levers layered each round port, and copper wind guards extended from the sides in an aviator style. "What you got in your backpack?" he growled.

I coiled back, but he clung harder, a silent threat to snap my arm. I kicked his shins, and he yelped, then shoved me away, my wrist still in his grip.

Chunk fell to the ground in hysterics. He stomped his feet like a toddler, and his belly flab jiggled. He finally sat up, legs splayed, and wiped his sleeve underneath his snotty nose. "She's a hoot, Sal!"

An object zinged by my head. It bounced off Chunk's temple. His eyes rolled up, and he fell backward in a heap.

"What?" Sal hauled me over to Chunk. "Get up, snucker. Quit messing around." He nudged Chunk with his boot.

I yanked my arm from Sal. It caught him off guard but not enough to free me. He flung his coat open and wrenched me close. A knife holstered to his belt jammed my hip. My legs gave out.

"Oh, no, you don't. Your bag is mine." Sal released my wrist but flung his arm around my middle. He heaved me onto his shoulder, knocking the wind from me.

I winced and raised my head to peer around his shoulder at Chunk. The view from atop Sal's frame gave me a fresh stream of barf waves. I should've let it blow all over him, but the fear of what he'd do to me squelched my gag reflexes.

Sal jabbed Chunk's side with his boot tip. "Let's go, you bloated whale." Not even a groan escaped Chunk's unconscious gaping mouth. "Boss is gonna be mad about this." He prodded Chunk again and muttered, "You was always the favorite. Load of garbage if you ask me."

My hip ached from the pressure of Sal's shoulder. I had to make a move while he was preoccupied. I brought my fists down on his back, but he held steady. I kicked my legs like a dolphin, knocking the air from my lungs.

"Enough!" Sal tossed me to the ground, sending me to my rear. "I'll deal with you now." Within seconds, he had his knife pointed between my eyes.

"Wait, I—" Adrenaline messed with all my circuits. I couldn't focus enough to form words.

Sal placed the sharp tip to my forehead, and my mind warped into a blank canvas. "Bye, bye, little girl."

My eyes shut tight. A picture of Mom, Dad, and Aunt Maria flashed. I'd never get to them.

THWACK!

I blinked open my lids. Sal lay splayed out next to Chunk. I scrambled to my feet and backed away. What the atom? I squelched the temptation to sneaker-check Sal's head. He appeared knocked out cold, but no sense testing fate and having him go all zombie on me. This world was getting way different from the one I'd written.

The skin on my arms rippled with bumps at a scuff sound behind me. I whirled around.

"Hello there, Miss."

6 Boxcar Home

A BOY MY age, a head shorter than me with a lopsided grin, stood with hands on hips. Upon his head of short, black curls rested a squat top hat with brown leather goggles around the base. A thick brass chain hung from his waist, adorned with several dangling pocket watches and a copper slingshot.

I grabbed my backpack straps and peered down at him as I side-stepped around Sal and Chunk's bodies.

The boy held up his arms. "Hey, wait. I won't hurt ya." He used one hand to loosen a red scarf around his neck. The blast of color popped out from the murky shades of his outfit. Dirt smudges across his cheeks matched the cocoa color of his long leather jacket. The frayed edges rippled in the breeze. He adjusted the strap of the leather satchel that crossed his chest, disturbing four small glass vials filled with a green liquid attached to his right breast pocket. He placed his hand over the vials to stop them from clinking.

Where'd he come from? Not from my story.

He lowered his hands. "Name's Mekasha." His voice cracked, and he thumbed at the unconscious bodies. "Seemed like ya needed help."

I opened my eyes wide at Sal and Chunk, then to the boy. "You did that?"

"Sure." He toyed with the slingshot. "Ya didn't think those two dropped from voodoo, did ya?" His chuckle broke into a smile.

I tried not to gawk at the long-gone tooth in the upper left side of his mouth. "No, not voodoo. Those guys are huge, and you're, um . . ."

"On the smaller side, yeah." Mekasha folded his arms. Gold chains swayed on the backs of his leather sleeves. "But ain't hard taking down a giant with a pebble." He winked. "Ya need to know the right spot."

"Uh, th-thanks. I . . . uh, I need to go." I turned away, worried he'd ask too many questions and slow me down.

"Wait. Nice goggles ya got there." He pointed to my socks. "Ya like the color orange? What's yer name? Where ya from?"

Well, that didn't work.

I stopped and pulled up my red sock, then my yellow. He was clever enough to figure out my favorite color, and he may have saved me from the would-be thieves, but I didn't have it in me for nicey-nice time. I spun around and found he held out a wool blanket.

"From my bag." He patted his satchel. "Ya need it more than I do."

I noticed the crisp air seeping through the loose knitting of Mom's sweater. I was cold but didn't want to owe him any favors.

He stared, waiting.

My icy skin won out, and I took the cloth, wrapping it around my shoulders. Guess I could tell him my name and a fake place I was headed.

"Uh, I'm Issy." I shuffled my feet. "On my way to the casino, for eh, bingo." Oh brother. Couldn't I come up with a better line? Some fiction writer I was.

"Casino?" His head cocked. "Ya mean the one in Brighton Beach? Ya be a long way from there. I can tell ya ain't from around. Come to my place, least for tonight?"

"Well, I . . ." No chance I'd go with a stranger, especially in this world.

He raised his hands. "Trying to help." Then his cheery eyes faltered, and he hesitated. "I know how it is to be alone. Been alone most my life."

A moment of his pain stretched between us, sending an ache down my spine. He was nothing like Sal and Chunk—maybe he wasn't so bad to trust. He had saved me, after all. If I wanted to survive tonight and help my parents, I needed somewhere warm and safe to stay. I could try for a sympathetic innkeeper, but night was coming fast, and Mekasha seemed to be the obvious choice. Jocko would do the same. "Okay." I hitched up my backpack. "But I'll follow from behind."

He grinned, then tipped his hat and twirled around on his boot heel. "Here we go, now," he called over his shoulder, then took off for the cobbled path.

I fell into step behind him, and we turned right at an old

brick building.

Down one block and around a corner, I gasped as we entered a wide street. The scene came to life like I'd written in my book. At least this part was accurate. Twenty-story skyscrapers, topped with American flags, lined each side of the road. Massive bronze gears attached to the structures' walls churned with brass pipe crisscrossed over the facades. Steam shot up their fronts and out the tops, creating a canopy of fog over the city. Merchants occupied the lower levels of the buildings. Each store had a fancy name sign illuminated by street lamps along the road like an airplane landing strip.

No way! There was my store! *Issy-Gadgetsporium* sat four shops away. Would all of my inventions be in there? I wanted to go inside, but no doubt Mekasha would start asking questions.

Woah! Is that? I shook my head at a pirate ship hovering in the sky a few buildings away. The masts reached the clouds, and the sails rippled in the wind. Oh, I didn't have one of those in my book. My imagination overloaded at the sights.

Mekasha popped up in front of me. "Hey, we need to get a move on." But before I could reply, his eyes grew wide at something over my shoulder.

"Hey, stop!" The shout came from close behind.

Mekasha pulled my elbow. "Let's go!"

We tore off along the road. I clutched the blanket ends around my neck with one hand, the cloth flapping behind like a superhero's cape, and my other hand smashed my goggles in place. My backpack bounced all over. I hoped *la mariposa* wouldn't be damaged.

Storefronts flashed by. The Cairo Café, a corset shop, the New

York Times. We darted through an alley, squeezing between two parked horse carriages. Mekasha motioned for me to crouch. He plucked his slingshot off his belt and loaded a red glass marble from his jacket pocket into the sling. With careful aim through the carriage wheel spokes, he paused at bootsteps falling hard nearby. Then he let the marble go.

ZING!

"Ow!" A shout and a thud.

Mekasha slinked from behind the carriage to check things out. A few moments later, he let out a low whistle. "Okay, it be clear."

I joined him to find his boot resting on the chest of his target. My eyes popped wide. "Sal," I said.

"Can ya believe he came for more?" Mekasha roared with laughter, slapping his knee like we were at a hoedown.

"Shhhhh. What if Chunk is near?"

"Nah, I got him good before. He's out cold." Mekasha stepped off Sal. "But let's go in case yer sweetheart does come around."

I gave him my best pout. He laughed it off and led me around the horse carriages into an empty side alley. His bootsteps echoed between the brick walls, a haunting rhythm, taking my mind to a dark place. If I'd arrived before my parents, were they still at home? Was I me back home? The strain of the paradox jumbled my head. I was thankful for the interruption of Mekasha's jolly whistled tune. I sang the familiar notes.

"Take me out to the baaalll game. Take me out to the crowd. Buy me some peanuts and—"

Mekasha spun on his heel. "How do ya know that song?"

"I, uh." Gosh, didn't everyone know it?

He chewed on his cheek, a brow raised. "That song doesn't come out until 1908."

1908? I eyed him. "Wait. Then how do *you* know it?"

"Hmmm." He ignored my question and nodded at my sneakers. "Interesting footwear ya go there. So, spill. Time and place of yer jump."

I shrugged, pretending I'd no clue what he meant, although my heart was pounding. No way I could tell him I'd time traveled. Had he time traveled?

"Okay, Issy. Ya win." His eyebrow crept higher. "Let's go."

A sigh of relief escaped my mouth. I'd dodged his question—for now.

We cruised a few more alleys, up a small hill, and through a trench to railroad tracks. Mekasha climbed the steps to the door of a rusty boxcar with "Lord and Taylor Department Store" painted on the side in faded blue. He worked a lock mechanism on the door by turning a wheel in a sequence of spins. A gear kicked into motion, triggering a set of pistons.

CLUNK. The door slid open.

"Come on up." Mekasha waved me to follow.

I headed up the rickety stairs. A melee of tick-tocks greeted me inside the boxcar. Mekasha threw his hat, satchel, and jacket over a tattered green armchair. He plucked a matchbook off the wall, struck a match on his vest, and lit a lantern.

Light saturated the cramped container, giving objects definition. An old mustard yellow couch sat on the far wall, opposite the ratty armchair, complete with a scratched-up sofa table and worn rug. An assortment of about two dozen clocks hung on the wall above the couch. Timepieces of varied sizes and shapes whirred with gears and pendulums. They displayed the same time down to the minute: 6:15 p.m. Mekasha must be serious about time.

A metal spiral staircase in the far right corner led to a loft over the couch. Blankets peeked through the wrought-iron bars at the loft's edge.

To my left, black and white photos covered the wall in crookedly hung frames. A man and woman, some with a young girl identical to Mekasha. Were they his family? The boxcar wasn't big enough for four people.

A large desk decorated with copper trim and brass knobs took over the right-hand wall. Papers, wires, gears, wrenches, and jars full of marbles covered its surface. I wanted to rush over to his workspace and start building. It was how I imagined my own space would look, minus the marbles. Way too many marbles.

The center of the desk held a large telescope. Its wide end pointed at a Petri dish-sized porthole cut into the boxcar wall.

Mekasha noticed my stare. "Ya want to try a look?"

I nodded, a chuckle tickling the corner of my mouth. I'd love to have a telescope.

Mekasha took the blanket from me, and I set my backpack near the door before joining him at the desk. I lifted one hand to the sleek black tube.

"Uh, ya need both hands to operate it," he said.

"Yeah, sure." I put my other hand on the tube, then hesitated. "Why are you so nice to me?" I said.

Mekasha flipped a few levers on the scope. "Because ya seem kind. Like me."

Like him? I wasn't like anybody. "People back home only pretend to be my friend."

"I'm not pretending, Issy." He dipped his head in a fancy way.

I liked the way he pronounced my name, *Is-say*. This boy seemed genuine—but no. "I don't have time for friends."

He leaned in. "Everyone needs chums. Friendship connects us all."

My words faltered. What did Mekasha want from me?

He clicked his tongue. "I can't say much about yer clothes, but yer goggles be great." His eyes narrowed. "Fits right into my *time*."

7 LUNA

MY EYES FROZE wide. Was his comment a hint that he knew about my time travel? Would he get in the way? I had to keep him out of my business. A warm place to sleep tonight was all I needed from him.

Mekasha ducked behind his desk, and I quickly shook the frazzled look off my face while he dragged out a trunk. He flipped open the lid, and a brown dust plume exploded in our faces. I sneezed into my arm.

He handed me a pair of rust-colored cotton pants with a waist-length leather jacket of the same shade. "Here, try these." Mekasha nudged the trunk with his boot. "Whatever else ya find in here, ya can have. All stuff I've collected in trades." He dipped out the boxcar door and closed it behind.

The musty leather jacket held the same scent as Dad's briefcase. I rummaged around the garments, pulling out a few more pieces, including a pair of short-heeled boots that appeared would fit. A thrill buzzed about me, trying on clothes I'd only seen in pictures. I wiggled a long-sleeved white collared blouse over my tank top. The material bunched around my wrists in ruffles. I layered on a fitted black suede vest and connected its three buckles up the center. Each buckle face held a copper gear with a small wire coil.

I flipped off my sneakers and slipped each leg into the loose pants, pulling them up over my shorts. A drawstring made it easy to cinch the top with the shirt tucked in. I squished the bottom of a pant leg into my red sock and did the same with the yellow one. Next, I slid my feet into the deep chocolate boots with gold chains swooping along their sides. I tightened the laces up to my mid-calf, and each sock peeked out the tops.

A full-length mirror behind the trunk reflected the almost completed outfit. I tucked into the leather jacket, and it fit me picture-perfect. I connected the single button at the waist, which allowed my vest to show from between the jacket lapels.

The mirror revealed an impossible-to-believe image. Shocking. I looked like a majestic 19th-century explorer. I wiggled my goggles atop my head. A slingshot sure would complete my look. A knock startled me.

"Issy, ya ready?" Mekasha said.

I smoothed down my hair. "Yeah, come in."

He stepped inside, his eyes meeting mine with an amused expression. Was he about to laugh at me? Had he tricked me into these clothes as a joke? My lips quivered.

Mekasha's face flashed with alarm. He strode over to me. "Oh, Issy, I'm sorry. I didn't mean to embarrass ya." He tapped

my hand.

I leaned away, unsure. He sounded sincere.

He closed his eyes a moment. "Ya reminded me of my sister. She loved dressing up."

"Where is your sis—"

"But ya." Mekasha flung his hand in the air, cutting me off. "Ya look terrific. And I have one more thing." Mischief played in his eyes. He retrieved something from the trunk. "Try it."

A mask. Like the decorative copper designs in my book. I'd always wanted one. I slipped it over my face, securing the velvet strap around my head. Velour lined the inside, giving it a plushness against my skin. I peered into the mirror and exhaled. The half-mask covered the right side of my face.

Swirly wire ran from my chin, up along my jawline, and over my cheek. It continued across my nose, my right eye, and covered my forehead. I peered out the peephole cut within the tight curls and swirls.

Mekasha's grin beamed in the mirror. I eyed my boots a moment, muttering to myself, "Stop it. You've known him all of two seconds. He's not an insta-buddy. Find Mom and Dad, get out."

Mekasha toyed with his slingshot. "Ya talking to yerself?"

"Oh, no, saying a little prayer. Grateful for the clothes and neat disguise."

"Face covers, goggles, mechanical arms. They're common around here. Need to make certain ya dress for *this* time." He gave an exaggerated wink.

Another hint. He knew my secret. I challenged him. "What do you know about time?"

"I study how the stars work with time, patterns, and such. My charts showed something a little off in the area near the docks. I was investigating when I found ya in yer weird clothes."

Maybe he did know about time travel and could help me. Nope, I couldn't risk it. Even if he did want to help, he might make a mistake. Tell someone my secret. I could end up in jail and miss saving my parents.

A topic change, quick. "Where are your parents?"

"They're dead," he said matter-of-factly.

My eyelids flew up. "I, I'm sorry."

"They died when I was eight. I've gotten used to being on my own." He stepped over to the desk and peered through the telescope. I did my best to hold my tongue for the ten seconds he held silent at the scope.

"Where's your sister?" I whispered, afraid of the answer.

Mekasha turned on his boot heel. "She's alive, but not sure *when* she is."

"When?"

His pocket watches clanked between his fiddling fingers. "Yeah, *when*. I've dabbled in time leaping, like ya." He smirked.

"I knew you knew." I finally gave in. No use pretending with Mekasha.

He smacked his knee, bellowing a laugh and sprawling on the sofa. "I knew ya knew I knew. Ya are a smart one. Now, with that out of the way, let's talk about how ya got here."

I plopped into the armchair, clicking my number rings to focus on calming my adrenaline, the hormone that triggers the body's fight-or-flight response. I didn't want to fight, and I had nowhere to flee. Deep breath. Let it out. Oxygen to the brain equals more energy for my neurons to calculate a way through this mess.

"It all happened so fast," I said. "I read the novel I wrote—"

Mekasha held up his hand. "Ya wrote a book?" He gave an opera performance-worthy clap. "Bravo. That is hard to do. My dad wrote a book on how to manage a barbershop. Didn't see him for months."

"Yeah, my first book. The strangest storm showed up a few weeks before my reading. That moment in front of my parents, the weather went wild. Then a burst of blue light struck my family room. The smoke cleared, and my parents were gone, sucked into a wormhole." I paused to allow Mekasha to respond to what must sound like a ridiculous story, but he leaned in, attentive, a silent urge to continue.

"I searched everywhere for my parents. Then I saw them. *Inside* my book." I expected a spectacular response from Mekasha. Instead, he popped up from his seat and skittered over to his desk.

"Interesting." He rummaged around a paper stack, speaking to himself. "Hmmm, inside a book. That's a new one." He looked at me. "Ya wrote this world?"

"I, I think so." But how could I have written an alternate reality into existence? "The world is similar, but the characters changed. Soldiers that I never wrote in dragged them away."

"Ah, the soldiers. We don't see them a lot around these parts of the city. Their main station is at the docks."

"The docks? No wonder they showed up fast after my parents came through."

Mekasha pinched his arm. "Hold on. If ya didn't write me into yer story, then does that mean I'm not real?" He chuckled at his joke. "Could ya have time traveled before and not remembered?"

"Trick question if I couldn't remember, right?" I pushed my mask tight to my face to give my hands something to do. "No. I wouldn't forget swirling inside a wormhole." And landing in a parallel universe.

Mekasha tapped his forehead. "Not everyone remembers. If the timeline gets reset, then the jumper could forget the travel."

"Reset?" I said.

"Yeah. Time Jumpers can travel to the past or future and change moments. Few do because it usually creates horrible outcomes. Timelines get reset and may cause folks to relive periods without memory of the original events."

"I've never time traveled before today. My parents discovered the wormhole not very long ago."

"Where are yer parents now?"

My head dropped. "Somewhere here? I don't know. I followed them, but by the position of the moon here right now, compared to the picture in my book . . ." I shrugged. "I arrived too early. They won't show up for another six nights."

Mekasha hopped to his feet and paced. He fiddled with his pocket watches, then stopped. "Where will their wormhole open?"

"At the docks. In front of the ship with the dedication banner for the Statue of Liberty."

He sat on the couch. "Okay, good. Now, let's figure out how the wormhole opened at yer house. Certain energies are needed."

"Like a tachyon?" I remembered the information on the flash drive.

Mekasha's head jerked up. "Ya know of tachyons?" His voice rose two octaves. "Did ya find any around yer house?"

"I'm not sure. I read about it in my parents' notes but no clue what they look like."

"Try to remember." He stared at me intensely. "Ya wouldn't be able to see them. They'd be inside something, stored, kept in a vessel."

"What makes you think there are tachyons at my house?" I said.

"Ya must have a large tachyon source to open a wormhole and a smaller vessel to take with ya to keep the hole stable."

"Ahhh." One logical place existed. "My parents' lab."

His eyes brightened. "A lab? Did ya see any containers made of metal? Something small can hold several hundred thousand tachyons."

"Hold on." I hopped up and snatched my backpack, then returned to the armchair. I showed him the glass jar. The mechanical butterfly stilled as I removed the lid. "Found her inside a puzzle box."

Mekasha dropped to his knees and scooted over. He tapped the jar. "Luna?"

"Wait, you know her?"

He nodded to my question but kept his eyes on Luna. She twitched a bit. Her antennae wiggled, and she clinked the glass with her feet. She crawled up the inside and perched on the rim, unfolding her crescent moon-decorated wings before taking flight around Mekasha's head.

He laughed in awe. "This is Luna. Issy, where'd ya find her?"

8 Bizarre

LUNA? AUNT MARIA would get a kick out of her favorite *mariposa's* name.

The silent reunion confused me but gave me a warm zing all the same. Mekasha beamed at Luna circling above. She landed on his shoulder, and he grinned like a five-year-old with cotton candy at a carnival.

"I've met Luna before." He jiggled his shoulder to show off the butterfly. "She has your tachyons."

"Really?" She looked like a motorized bug to me. "Where are they?"

Mekasha held out his hand, and Luna glided down to his palm. "Her eyes."

I leaned in, mesmerized by the dark lenses. My arm hairs raised, and an iridescent trail swirled inside her orbs. "Like pools of water with oil floating on top."

"What do ya feel?" Mekasha said. He inched his hand closer.

I touched her wing, and my skin prickled. "An energy. Like when I first found her."

"Yeah." He focused on Luna. "Ya are feeling the force of the tachyons stored in her eyes. She's a small vessel. Not enough to open a wormhole but plenty to have kept it stable when ya came through. Some other stronger tachyon source at yer house opened it."

Maybe Whiz was the main source? I'd no clue, but at least Luna had tachyons. Relief melted my shoulders as she pranced around Mekasha's hand. "I can use her to keep my parents' wormhole stable when they arrive."

Mekasha frowned. "No, ya can't." His voice came out forced.

"Why not?" I reached for her. "She's my butterfly." Who did he think he was?

He placed Luna on the coffee table and folded his arms. His demeanor changed to ready-for-an-argument-Mekasha. "She's not yer butterfly. I need the tachyons."

I tore off the mask. "Why? You study time. I want to go home!" He was using me for Luna's tachyons.

He sat back on the couch and squeezed his hands together, finally letting out a long sigh. "Issy, I'm sorry. Of course, ya need to get home. I can wait."

His sad eyes bristled my spine. "Why do you want the tachyons so bad?"

"My sister. She's out there, somewhere, sometime."

I gulped. "What happened to her?"

"My fault." Mekasha let out a breath. "Three years ago, I was messing with tachyons. A wormhole opened, sucked her in."

He gazed at the floor. "She had a little bit of tachyons stored in a pocket watch we'd found, but not enough to get her back home. I need more to time jump and save her."

I clicked my number rings, my heart aching for him. There had to be a way. "Let's share Luna's tachyons. We'll put some into another vessel."

Mekasha shook his head. "A vessel can't be opened. Tachyons will spread and lose energy. Ya must take the whole vessel."

I slumped back in the armchair. My family didn't belong here. I wanted to help him, but if I didn't keep hold of Luna, 1886 would be our permanent home. "I'm not sure what to do. If I have Luna, how did my parents get through the wormhole?"

"They must've had a tachyon source too. Could be a big enough one for all of you to use."

The scene of my family room flashed before me. No vessel anywhere. "All they had were the clothes on their backs."

Mekasha shrugged. "They had something."

"What if you jump with Luna to get your sister?" I said. "Then, you come back, and I use Luna?" It was such an easy plan.

"Issy." He paused for several seconds.

"What?" His puppy-sad eyes stung my heart.

"Each jump uses energy. Luna might not have enough to get my sister and me back here. Even now, Luna maybe doesn't have the strength to take yer family home."

"That can't be right. She had plenty to get me here, and she's totally fine."

Luna clicked her wings and wiggled her antennae.

Mekasha placed his hands in a prayer position. "I do want

ya all to get home. But the more folks in a jump, the more tachyons needed. Luna is a small vessel, maybe strong enough for one more trip with two people."

I squished myself into the chair cushions. I had to keep Luna. She was my only way home, enough energy or not. But, Mekasha needed her, too. How would we decide who got her? Or did we have to?

I gave my hands one hard clap. "Let's find more tachyons."

Mekasha clicked his tongue against the gap in his upper teeth. "I haven't found more vessels."

"Where do tachyons come from?"

"They travel to Earth through lightning bolts." Mekasha zig-zagged his finger in the air.

Had Whiz blasted our house with tachyons? "Can we catch them?"

Mekasha grabbed the back of his neck and squeezed. "That's the hard part. Ya can't see tachyons because they move faster than the speed of light. I don't know how to catch them, and Boss has goons hunting for any remaining vessels. Word on the street is some mysterious guy is giving Boss competition. Professor ain't much help either."

"Boss and Professor?"

His face lit up. "Professor is a brilliant man—"

I cut him off. "What's his name?"

"Professor."

"Huh? Just Professor? Not Professor Milligan or Professor Bob?"

Mekasha chuckled. "Nope. Professor."

"Like Cher, Madonna, Prince?"

"Uh." His forehead knitted.

I waved my hand. "Never mind, go ahead." I smiled at how easy it was to talk with Mekasha. Like I'd known him forever. But I had to remember: he wanted Luna, and I wanted to get home.

"Professor is smart about time travel. He told me once that he had three stashes of tachyons, one being Luna."

"Luna belongs to Professor?"

"Yeah."

Great. Professor might want Luna back. "Where are his other two stashes?" I said.

Mekasha rubbed his chin. "Professor can't remember where they are or the vessels he used."

"That's pretty important information."

"He don't have all his marbles." Mekasha pointed to his head. "Time leap overdose," he said, like everyone and their dog knew what "time leap overdose" meant.

I gave him a blank stare. "Uh, huh."

"Professor leaped too many times without my *Tempus-Viator* potion." Mekasha reached for his jacket on the armchair and unclipped a small glass vial off the chest pocket. He held up the green fluid. "A mix of herbs and minerals to protect the body from time travel brain scramble."

"Brain scramble?" I squeezed my eyes shut a second. "Could I lose my marbles from my leap?"

"Ya should be okay with a couple of trips as long as yer body gets rest."

Good. The last thing I needed was my brain going to mush. "You made the liquid?" I said.

"Yeah." He re-clipped the vial to his jacket. "Lots of research about homeopathy, natural healing."

"Have you made anything else?" I had to keep Mekasha's mind off his sister and his need for *my* butterfly. A tinge of guilt poked me. Who was I becoming? I'd always helped people, not hurt them. But couldn't he track more tachyons after I left for home?

"Sure, I've made lots of things." He threw his finger into the air, jabbing through my thoughts. "Let me show ya."

"Yeah, sure." I followed him to his desk.

Mekasha removed a towel off a small cabinet about the size of an upright shoebox. Gears and levers covered the dark metal on each side of the closed door. He turned a center handle several times. Steam spurted from behind the cabinet while gears kicked into motion on the right side.

The cabinet door cranked open to an empty cavity except for a small spout on the rear wall. A glass dropped from the cabinet ceiling and landed below the spout. Mekasha pushed a sequence of levers, which sent the steam higher, and caramel tinted liquid flowed into the glass a third of the way up.

With a couple more pulls of the levers, steam gushed, and air spit from the spout before bubbly water filled the glass. Gears on the side turned, and the platform lurched forward. Halfway out the cabinet door, the glass stopped.

"Still working out the kinks." He handed me the glass. "Here, ya go."

I took a sip, and soda bubbles sprinkled my nose. A rush of bubbly exploded in my mouth. "Wow! You made this?"

"Yeah. Fizzy pop." Mekasha puffed his chest. "Gives yer step a pep."

I held the glass up in a toast. "Good stuff." I pointed to the gears on the cabinet. "Hey, I can help you fix it, so the glass comes out."

Mekasha handed me a screwdriver. "Be my guest."

I tightened the screws in the center of a couple of gears and loosened the screws in others, then signaled Mekasha to trigger the machine. The platform came out fully, serving us another glass of fizzy pop.

Amazement sparked behind his eyes. "How'd ya do that?"

"Math. I counted the gear rotations when you made the first drink and noticed some gears moved too fast, some too slow. They stopped because they jammed up. A quick calculation on the number of rotations versus the approximate size of each gear to adjust their speeds."

"Incredible. Ya are a math genius."

I laughed. "I'm not a genius, but I do have a habit of making things into a math problem. But don't tell my mom." I took my drink to the couch. "Where do you think Professor put the tachyon stashes?"

Mekasha leaned against the desk's edge. "Hard to say. Professor's been all over this city."

A nagging thought hovered at my brain's edge. How did Luna end up in my parents' lab? And if there was one butterfly with tachyons, could there be . . . "Maybe Professor made similar butterflies?"

"Possible." Mekasha moved to the sofa table and picked up Luna. "An incredible clockwork butterfly, an automaton." Luna flicked her wings in response.

"Is she alive?" I said. Surely not, but I couldn't help ask.

Luna seemed way more than bits and parts.

"Some might say Luna has a personality. I always thought it my imagination. Professor must've learned how to make her during his travels to the future."

"Amazing invention." I reached out, and Luna sprung up, flitting over to my wrist. A zing tingled my skin. "I think she likes me." She waved a wing in my direction, then flew off and settled atop the telescope. "We should find other stashes."

Mekasha faced the wall of tick-tock clocks. "Believe me. I've tried. Boss has too many goons out there snatching 'em up."

The excitement over Professor's tachyons fell a notch. "Who's this Boss?"

"Boss runs the underground and is ruthless at taking all tachyons. Ya remember Sal and Chunk? They work for Boss, searching the city for tachyons. That's why they still came for ya after I knocked 'em out."

"What do you mean?"

He nodded at my backpack. "Sal and Chunk have a tachyon detector. It detects the presence of tachyons within about a half-mile. Then they hunt the spot."

"I saw it on Sal's belt, all whirring, carrying on. That's why he went for my bag."

"Yeah. He likely figured ya had tachyons in it, but the detector ain't precise. I'm working on a more powerful one that gives the exact location."

An invisible string of camaraderie tightened between us. "That's a cool invention." I wished Mekasha went to my school. For now, we had an impossible task here in 1886. "Why does Boss want all the tachyons?"

"Boss is a Time Pirate. Jumping here and there to steal riches. More tachyons equal more jumps." He strolled over to his telescope and peeked through the lens. "Controlling all the tachyons means less competition from other Time Jumpers." His voice broke. He turned to me and shook his head. "Leaving no tachyons to find my sister."

I held up a finger. "But there are other sources. We find Professor. Help him to remember where he hid the other two stashes."

"Don't know about that, Issy." Mekasha folded his arms. "Professor's had a rough life. He avoids talking about time travel now. He has taken to being alone."

"I understand wanting to be alone. But we have to find him. The waxing gibbous moon is in less than a week. I must be on the docks with tachyons when my parents arrive."

Mekasha closed his eyes a moment, then clicked his tongue. "Okay, Issy, we go look for him."

I grabbed my backpack and slipped out my book, flipping the pages, searching for other places I'd created. "Could Professor be at the Bizarre Bazaar?"

Mekasha slapped his knee. "How'd ya hear of the Bizarre Bazaar?"

"I wrote it. Jocko goes there to find clues about his suspects."

He angled his chin up at me. "Ya are an interesting friend."

I gulped, and my cheeks blazed. People never called me that. I searched his expression for a hint of fakeness, but his face beamed as if nothing else mattered.

"Professor owns a tent at the bizarre," Mekasha said. "He may be there."

I grabbed my bag. "Let's go."

"Hold on. It seems like maybe yer book is a little different than this place. Ya may find our bazaar, eh, a bit rougher at night than the one ya wrote about."

I pursed my lips, but he was probably right. This world was similar to the one in my story, except some stuff here was scarier. Like the soldiers who took Mom and Dad. "Okay then, tomorrow morning we go to the Bizarre Bazaar."

9 SKULL

THE NEXT DAY, I woke to a symphony of tick-tocks. The many timepieces chimed the current hour: four o'clock in the afternoon! I'd slept all night and half the day. I rolled to the loft's edge for a view, finding Mekasha sorting a stack of papers on his desk. He had given me the bed while he'd slept on the couch.

I scrabbled out from the warm blankets and called over the loft edge, "Mekasha, why didn't you wake me?"

"Ya needed rest." He tossed me a small bread roll as I descended the stairs. I plopped onto the couch, nibbling the meager meal.

"Thanks," I said, my hungry growl sharper than I'd planned. "You know we don't have much time. I didn't need to sleep that long."

"Time travel is hard on yer body." His voice turned grim. "I had to let ya rest. Don't want to risk brain—" He gritted his teeth.

"Brain scramble?" I shivered. "Okay, I understand. Thanks for doing that." My chest lightened. He cared about what happened to me. "Are we still good with the bazaar this late?"

"We should have enough light to walk there then be gone before it gets too wild. I'll bring extra marbles." He patted the slingshot at his waist.

I finished my meal, took a fast break outside behind a bush, then came back to dress and fetch my backpack.

Mekasha slipped into his leather jacket, patting down his vials and pocket watches. "Now, our Bizarre Bazaar is where everyone goes to trade and sometimes steal." His exaggerated wink made me laugh. He ducked into the strap of his satchel and put on his top hat, goggles snug above the hat's brim. Lantern light danced off the lenses like little white bursts winking at me, too.

I loaded Luna into Mekasha's satchel, safe inside her jar. "Professor trades stuff there?"

"Yeah, he used to make trinkets to sell." Mekasha's eyes fell. "All he remembers how to do, what with the brain scramble. Hopefully, he'll be there."

I hadn't met Professor, but the story of his trinket-making life created a pit in my core. What was life without our memories?

Mekasha blew out the lantern and opened the boxcar door. A chilled breeze hit me in the face. I pulled my jacket tight and put on my mask. He followed me out and slammed the door shut. The lock reset in a reversed sequence.

Gloomy clouds made it darker outside than the late afternoon hour. We trudged toward the outskirts of New York City, weaving through dank brick-walled alleys to the corner of 14th street and 6th avenue.

Burgundy-bricked structures lined either side of the long boulevard, lit by gas-burning street lamps, haloed within the steam clouds. The reddish-browns made it all look like an animated, old-time photo.

Passing R.H. Macy & Co., I couldn't help peek at my reflection in the store windows. The dark rust leather jacket and pants, black vest, and copper-wired mask all worked together to turn me into something magical. I looked so different but in a good way. The goggles atop my head held my hair back. I inched up my chin. The mask gave me confidence I hadn't known before. Here, I fit in. Steampunk, science, and all.

I strode at Mekasha's side in step with the rhythmic click of distant train wheels over tracks. My nose twitched at the smoky scent of burnt coal. A constant drone hummed around us from steam-powered machines on the street corners. Some devices held chairs where customers sat with their mechanical arm braces being polished by workers. The women's outlandish outfits rivaled the best Halloween stores at home.

A sausage cart, powered by a steam-spewing water pump, roasted franks on a set of rolling bars. I did a double-take at the mechanical monkey wearing miniature goggles and a tiny leather jacket. He poured teacup after teacup of water into a funnel over the pump.

Above us, hundreds of automaton hummingbirds zoomed in and out between people, snatching up trash and dropped scraps. The walkways were cleaner than my kitchen floor back home.

"Can we buy some food?" I pleaded to Mekasha.

"Yeah, we will." He shrugged. "Sorry I couldn't offer more

at the boxcar. I'm limited on supplies."

"It's fine," I said, although my mid-section squelched in protest.

We continued on 14th near the pubs. Piano keys clattered, and accordions wheezed out the doors. A rush of gratitude for my new friend came out of nowhere when Mekasha steered me from the path of a drunken man. I peeked at Mekasha. He was more like me than anyone I knew back home, into inventing and sciences about the unknown.

"Stop it," I whispered to myself. "Focus on the tachyons."

Mekasha side-eyed me, but I diverted his attention to a storefront. "Hey, look, cakes."

A bakery taunted us with its hot oven swirling fresh apple pie aroma out the open window. Next door, the baggage repair shop displayed leather suitcases in a light bulb-framed window, while the G.E.O. C. Flint Co. showcased handsome leather couches and wing-backed chairs fashioned with mechanical headrests. Dad would've loved one of those chairs. A good "thinking" chair, he'd call it.

I got a kick out of people's outrageous masks covering most of their faces, reaching up past their foreheads in intricate designs. My favorite was a copper-wired peacock shimmering in blue greens. The scariest—a bronze mask shaped like a skull, complete with empty black eyes above a hollow nose and jagged yellow teeth set in a permanent grin. I hustled away from the Skull man.

"Ya okay, Issy?" Mekasha said.

"Yeah, I'm good." I stiffened, craning my neck at Skull as he clomped past. He cursed under his breath and tapped a small black box on his belt.

Mekasha must have caught the horror etched in my eyes. "Nothing to worry about. Folks enjoy their masks here. Now, let's get some eats."

We crossed the street, and a clockwork horse stopped in my path. I dug in my heels to avoid a headbutt on its metal-sheeted haunches. He snorted mist and pawed at the ground, horseshoes clicking on stone. The rider shoved a lever then smacked the horse's side with his gloved hand. "Go on, then," he said to the beast. The horse raised its tail.

I hurried to avoid the plop-plop of the horse's business, and instead, a steam cloud gushed from its rear. The spray missed me by inches, and I laughed. Like a clockwork horse would have a digestive system to create road apples.

We arrived at a food trolley filled with pastries surrounded by stacks of grilled cheese sandwiches. A hefty woman in a stained apron shouted prices from behind the display. Her arms flew like a tangle of tentacles, tossing out food to the crowd and taking money. Mekasha strutted briskly, eyes straight ahead, hands in his pockets. We neared the end of the cart.

"Wait, why aren't we stop—"

Mekasha held up his palm. He lifted two sandwiches in a maneuver that somehow landed the delectable items into his satchel with two glass marbles taking their spots on the cart.

My brows shot up. "What the atom?"

Mekasha strolled the sidewalk, and I hurried after him. The woman paid no attention as we circled a corner and stopped in a dark alley.

"Did we steal those sandwiches?" I said.

"Ya think I stole those?" Mekasha gave an over-the-top sigh.

"I'm hurt, Issy. How could ya?"

I laughed, and my mask jiggled. "Okay, fancy-pants actor. I've known you what, a few hours? You left marbles instead of money."

He motioned toward two wooden crates, offering me the first pick. I chose the least dirty and waited for his explanation.

"Look, I'm an orphan. No money, no skills." He tapped the side of his head. "But I'm street smart. I survive so I can find my sister."

My bones ached with the heaviness of his life. I wished I had some fancy words of encouragement, but the truth was I understood. If I couldn't save my parents, then what? Family was the most important thing.

He handed me a sandwich. "For the first time in a long time, I have hope. Ya give me hope."

"Me?" I popped a piece of crust into my mouth.

"Yeah. I've searched a long time for tachyons. And here ya fall into my time with a supply of yer own. We can't both use Luna, but yer confidence with helping Professor find his stashes has given my step a pep." He clicked his boot heels together.

"And here I thought your fizzy pop gave you that." I raised my hand in an imaginary toast.

"Cheers." He took a bite of his sandwich, chewing like a horse with a mouthful of carrots. "Now," *chew, chew,* "about these grilled cheezies ya think I swiped," *chomp, chomp, swallow,* "do ya know anything about glass marbles?"

"Um, yeah, Mom uses them to decorate our plant containers. And she wears a big cat's eye around her neck."

"Marbles in the plants? Oh, they're too valuable for that."

"Valuable?" I said.

"Here in 1886 are only clay marbles. No glass ones yet. Big time making of glass marbles don't come around until 1915."

Calculations flew through my mind. "Wait, that's almost thirty years from now. How'd you—" I stopped at his sly snicker. "Ohh."

He nodded. "I picked 'em up in Ohio on a jump to 1915 Akron. Had to get outta there fast. The new General Tire company tried to hire me." He fished around his pocket and pulled out two silver marbles. "I have magnetic ones, too."

"You use them for money here?"

"Not too often if I can help it." He took another bite of his cheesy. "Don't want folks getting suspicious. Start nosing around on where the marbles come from. I've seen a few of 'em in the pawnshops for five dollars." He shoved the rest of the sandwich in his mouth, cheeks full-faced hamster.

"Five dollars." I tried to remember what I'd learned in history class about inflation. "It'd be like over one hundred in my time." Gosh, Mom had a gold mine in her vases. Each vase had a circumference of about five inches, filled with half-inch marbles—

Mekasha clapped his hands clean of crumbs, bringing me out of the math problem. "Let's get on our way. The Bizarre Bazaar isn't a polite place when the city pubs close."

I adjusted my mask, hefted my backpack, and walked beside Mekasha up a side street. We emerged near a corner church where I grasped his arm, unable to speak.

"Issy, what's wrong?" Mekasha followed my gaze.

Skull, on the church steps, turned his wicked grin on us.

10 Q-Tip Legs

MEKASHA HELD HIS hand across his chest. "Ya scared me, Issy. I thought ya got hurt."

"I, but." I looked back at the steps. Wait. What? Skull was gone. Had he slipped around the corner? "Skull was there."

Mekasha took my elbow and guided me underneath a street lamp. The glow washed over me like a safe cocoon. Or maybe Mekasha's presence made me feel protected? I mean, I'd only met him yesterday, but somehow, it felt like forever.

"Skull is following us," I said to Mekasha.

"Ya named him Skull? Good one." He chuckled and patted my shoulder. "Issy, ya will see interesting masks. Skulls, animals, clowns. All in fun. It's normal."

Normal. I was so different that I didn't know what normal was.

But I liked my mask, even if it didn't feel normal yet. Beneath it, I could be anything I wanted, and no one judged. But, Skull.

I was sure his mask reflected who he was, and it scared me.

"Ready?" Mekasha tapped my shoulder.

"Yeah, one second. May I?" I pointed to Mekasha's satchel, and he opened the flap. Luna wiggled her antennae at us from inside the glass jar. "Good girl. You hang tight."

We headed into the church's backfield, maneuvering over pumpkins and their vines. I eyed Mekasha. He'd done me a favor, taking me to find more tachyons when he needed them, too. Wasn't that what a friend would do? I forced myself not to think of him as that word. If we couldn't find another vessel, then we'd have to decide who got Luna. An awful decision.

I stomped forward, and a furry something skittered by my feet. I shuddered with the heebie-jeebies, leaping to avoid the creature, at which Mekasha offered his booming laugh.

I displayed my "yeah-so-funny" smirk. "Haha."

Beyond the church graveyard, we entered an open field with low hills. A milky glow hovered above the horizon. Fireworks burst in the inky sky, giving off a faint sulfur odor. They cracked off blue, yellow, and pink streams before sizzling from sight.

"We're close. This is how I pictured it in my book."

Excitement sparked his eyes. "I can't wait to see how yer world compares to ours. Our bazaar might be more lively than ya wrote about."

"So you said." I grinned.

We marched across the field, up a slope to the hilltop. The glow turned into a flood of illumination. Hundreds of strung lightbulbs crisscrossed between bunched-up circus-like tents in reds, blues, and yellows. People packed the spaces between the marquees. They milled about, clanking metal cups together.

Twangs of violins and jittery tambourines collided with goat neighs and pig squeals in a clash of celebration. Yep. Way more fun than my bazaar.

Mekasha swept out his arm. "Welcome to the Bizarre Bazaar." He yanked down his goggles, giving the illusion of bug eyes under a top hat. I choked on my giggle as we clomped the last few feet to the bazaar's fringes.

Inside the festival, rambunctious crowds wore masks, some hideous, some fantastical. Mechanical arm pieces and oversized spectacles adorned the party-goers. Mekasha was right. The people, the steampunk outfits, the machines—way more imaginative than in my story. Doubt over my writing skills tugged at my confidence. I pushed it aside to enjoy the organized chaos around us.

An eagerness enveloped me. I wanted to be amongst the bizarre with the flawed characters I'd written, like me. And the outfits—from bird-like hoodies to a silver octopus head cap complete with tube tentacles. No doubt the bazaar lived up to its name. People flaunted their freedom to represent the title.

"Ya stay close. Merchant's Maze is easy to get lost in."

"Merchant's Maze?" I said. Oh, I was so using that in my book edits.

"Yeah, the tents where folks barter. No planning at all. Long rows, short rows, dead ends."

"I didn't put an unorganized market in my story." The differences stumped me. Why wouldn't it match my novel if I was the one who wrote this place into existence?

Mekasha tilted his head. "Yet somehow yer imagination came up with pieces from my world. I don't know, Issy, but we'll figure it out. Now, in Merchant's Maze, we use landmarks to gauge location."

He motioned me over to a knife stand with racks of steel blades, each gripped by decorative handles.

"Issy, if we get separated, meet here at Cutter's Cut. Ya can't miss the flying flags stamped with knife pictures. They are the tallest of all things at the bazaar."

The maroon and black flags flapped like water up against a boat. I lowered my eyes, startled to find a man staring at me. His beady eyes glowered from under a leather mask, covering his forehead down to the bridge of his nose.

"I's take care of you." Spittle flew from Mr. Beady's mouth. He gripped an old-fashioned coin dispenser at his waist next to three knives in slots around his belt.

"Move on, Gus." Mekasha fingered his slingshot. "She's with me."

Somehow, under his hat and goggles, Mekasha's scowl screamed, *don't mess with us.*

Gus slinked back a few steps. "Hold your pants there, slingshot-boy. This gal is my pal."

What? I shook my head.

Mekasha's jawline hardened. "Leave her alone. Understand?"

Gus glared, nodded, then turned to a customer in a gold cat mask with wired whiskers.

I stared at Mekasha. "What's his deal?"

"Gus claims to know all the girls at the bazaar. All talk." He held a pocket watch from his belt. "Close to five o'clock. Let's get to Professor's old tent."

He led me from Cutter's Cut by the hand, and we snaked around the crowd. Out of habit, I looked for patterns, counting the

tents, the turns we made, the rows we intersected, the merchants, and tucked the numbers into my memory.

Mekasha released my palm. He got out two sets of leather gloves from his satchel, giving one to me. "Getting colder."

Again, with the what-a-friend-would-do stuff. My skin goosied with bumps. How could I take Luna from him if we didn't find more tachyons?

We tugged on our gloves and continued filing between the people. Laughter, curse words, loud music, the spurts of steam. I stopped a moment, letting it all fill my ears like a chaotic melody. I wanted to memorize every sound so I'd have the perfect words to describe it in my story revision.

"Mekasha, what do you say—" I turned and scanned for his top hat. Gone. "Mekasha!" The mayhem swallowed my shout, and I couldn't see over the mass of heads. My throat tightened. Where had he said to meet him if we separated? Clever Cuts? No, no. Ghastly Gus's? I squeezed my eyes shut. Flag images flapped by. "Cutter's Cut."

I backtracked. Mental math helped me remember the number of tents we'd gone by plus the turns. The crowd was hard to maneuver, with some costumes having spiked tips. My best chance was to swim the Bizarre Bazaar. I hunched over and brought my hands up and out in a prayer position, cutting a path between people's waists. An open spot appeared, and I broke through the wave, but my heart thumped me with the old one-two punch. Skull!

He loitered thirty feet away at a merchant's table display, inspecting the black box hanging from his belt. His head shot up, the sharp edge of his mask coming into view. He stomped forward, his ghoulish eyes set on me. I wasn't about to hang around to see what he wanted. I skirted clusters of people, but Skull's strides closed the gap. A row of hanging tapestries at a rug tent gave me refuge, and I slipped inside, wedging between two thick mats.

Skull's bootsteps halted.

The musty carpets made me gasp for air. I held my hand with my number rings over my mouth to stifle the sounds. After several seconds of Skull remaining silent, I peeked out. He stood at the neighboring tent, banging his knuckles against the little black box and muttering about tachyons. Oh! He was hunting for sources. But why come after me? I wasn't carrying any. Luna was with Mekasha.

Skull's sunken eyes searched, his jagged breaths coming out in growls. He twisted his head side-to-side like a stiff-necked wooden puppet, then slammed the black box against his thigh and marched away.

I pushed out from my spot. Fabric frantically flapped above. There! The knife flags high over the next aisle. I dodged the more massive crowd until skidding to a stop at Cutter's Cut.

Gus's eyes bugged out at me, and his lips slithered into a sly smile. "Nice of you to return. Want to come inside for a sippy of something?"

"I'd rather fly into the ozone layer without protective gear." I narrowed my eyes in a harsh scowl. Gus was too friendly for my liking.

He squished up his forehead. "What's that supposed—" Before Gus could finish, his mouth clamped shut. A silver marble ricocheted off his noggin and landed on the counter. The magnetic ball rolled and connected to a nearby knife. He rubbed the spot between his eyes. "Hey, slingshot-boy," he snarled. "You could've knocked out my eye."

I spun around.

Mekasha. Goggles up around his hat's brim, slingshot aimed straight on. "Ya forget, Gus. I never miss my target." He lowered his weapon and eyed me. "What happened? One moment ya there, the next, gone."

"I'm sorry. I stopped for a minute."

"It was more than a minute. Anyway, stay by my side."

I fiddled with my mask, worried I'd disappointed him. "I will. And hey, Skull followed me. It looked like he had a tachyon detector on his belt."

Mekasha clicked his tongue. "He was after ya? But ya ain't carrying tachyons. His detector must be way off target. Sounds like the guy who's giving Boss competition."

"I'm not sure. He seemed determined to get to me. But then he got near my hiding spot and started hitting the detector like it wasn't working."

"He must've lost the tachyon signal. Let's go before ya run into any more trouble."

We left Gus's tent and re-entered the noisy bazaar crowd. Drinks spilled, people shoved, fireworks shot off at random. I dodged the scariest clown ever—spikey metal gears around each eye, sharp screws for teeth, a blood-red nose. No fun, in my opinion.

Mekasha kept us moving through the maze, calling out landmarks. I counted each tent and stored the route in my head.

"Right at the Satchel Station." He pointed. "Left at the

deep-fried caramel apples."

"Deep-fried apples. With caramel?" My mouth watered. Aunt Maria could help me whip up a batch of those once I got back to my world.

We maneuvered a few more turns, ending at a gray-stained tent. The sides sagged, and several frayed ropes lay in pieces around the edges. Mekasha approached the tent entrance, a simple slit up the middle, and pushed through.

I paused at the threshold, my arm shooting up across my nose. The scent of wet-dog-who'd-romped-in-a-pond-of-dead-fish hit me. I held my breath to avoid puking. A single lantern burned in the corner of the tent. A form in an overstuffed chair took shape within the shadows, the lump of a hunched man. The man reached and turned the lantern higher.

"Hey ya, Professor," Mekasha said.

The time travel genius sat there in his odd glory: short fiery hair stuck out in all directions, a gear-strewed leather jacket hanging from limp shoulders, paired with pink boxer shorts over Q-tip-thin legs. My hope in finding tachyons was in *this* guy?

11 A Daughter

"WELL, I'LL BE a hairless hamster." Professor pushed himself up from the rickety chair. He shuffled in worn-out slippers, his eyes shining like a proud father. "It's been a while, boy." He extended his hand. He couldn't be much older than Dad, but he moved slow. Had brain scramble done this?

"Professor." Mekasha gave a gentle shake. "How ya been?"

"Better than the bread-stealing rat." He swiped his thumb across his long, pointed nose.

"Where is the rat now?" Mekasha looked down at his boots.

Professor bent over and took the lid off a stew pot. The pot sat atop a small brick oven with a vent pipe running up and out a hole in the tent top. I about upchucked in my mouth from the odor.

"He's dinner tonight. Won't be stealing from no one anymore." Professor raised his finger at me. "Isadora."

My eyes widened behind my mask. "How do you know my name?"

"Oh, um." Professor's gaze darted around the tent. "No, no, I don't know *your* name."

"But ya said it." Mekasha ogled at him.

Professor picked up a book from the floor and waved it around. "Here. The author is Isadora, something or another. Must've had the name on my mind." He tossed the book behind him into a pile of socks. "What is your name, young lady?"

I scrunched my nose at Mekasha before addressing Professor. "I'm Issy. Nice to meet you." I gave a small wave then tucked my hands in my pockets to avoid shaking his touched-a-rat-palm.

"Pleasure's all mine, Issy." Professor scratched the red stubble on his chin.

"Professor, we've plenty to tell ya," Mekasha said. "Have a seat."

"I'm always up for a delightful story, boy. Keeps the brain young." Professor side-stepped around the stew pot and pulled out two stools. He handed them to Mekasha, who set the seats before Professor's chair, and we sat.

While Professor settled into his rocker, it gave me a few seconds to study the layout of his tent and maybe spy a possible tachyon vessel. A wide bookcase lined the canvas wall behind him. Cubbies held hardback books and various knickknacks. Smack dab in the middle of the top shelf was a framed photo of three young girls in pastel dresses sitting on a picnic bench.

"All right, let's get to it," Professor said, sitting wide-legged in his sleep shorts.

"Uh, trousers?" Mekasha motioned to Professor's lower half

as he took off his satchel and set it on the ground between us.

"Of course. Where are my manners?" He flipped off his slippers and nipped a pair of pants from the chair. After tugging them on, he hopped in place to pull up the waist before sitting. He rotated his hand a few times to signal Mekasha to carry on.

Mekasha leaned forward. "Professor, Issy is not from around here."

"She's not? Her mask and goggles perfectly fit in."

"What I mean," Mekasha said, "is that Issy is not from our *time*."

Professor's distant stare fell beyond Mekasha, and his blue eyes dulled. His trembling lips mumbled something.

I furrowed my brow at Mekasha, and he waved his hand. "Give him a moment. He's trying to remember something."

Professor broke into a song. "White string can make you sing all the daylong day." He cut off and focused on Mekasha. "You were saying?"

Mekasha closed his eyes a moment. "Issy traveled a wormhole to follow her parents. She needs tachyons to get her family home." He paused. "I also need tachyons to find Naya."

Professor sang, "Tie it, trap it, capture it with string and fling." His voice faded off, and he gazed at the picture of the girls.

"What's he doing?"

"He breaks out in this song whenever I mention time travel or Naya. He feels responsible for her because it was his tachyons I used."

I gasped. I'd been so worried about my family that I hadn't asked his sister's name. "Naya is a nice name."

"Yeah." His cheeks rose, almost touching the corners of his eyes. "We turn thirteen next month, the day after Thanksgiving."

"S-she's your twin." They were likely super close. Of course, he'd want Luna for the tachyons.

He nodded, then turned to Professor with a clap of his hands in front of the slackened face. "Think, Professor. Where did ya hide the tachyons?"

Professor pursed his lips with his hand held up. He counted each finger. "One potato, two potatoes, three potatoes, four, five potatoes." Raindrops tapped the tent tarp above, and the crowd outside whooped louder. Professor continued counting.

Mekasha huffed. "He can't focus when it comes to time travel."

"Why? What makes him go into this?" I hitched my thumb at the carrot-topped genius.

"After so many years of jumping, it's like his brain moves into protection mode."

"What about his past?"

"He won't talk about it. I used to see him a lot, but he stopped coming around to find me a couple of years ago." Mekasha sagged against the chair. "Wasn't much himself anymore."

I stood and walked to the bookcase, grabbing the photo of the three girls, each with strawberry-blonde tresses. Sitting back down, I held up the picture to Professor. "Who are they?"

Professor froze, hands mid-air, eyes darkening.

"White string can make you sing all the daylong day."

Rain fell harder, echoing my frustration with the situation. I didn't have time for these puzzles. We had to find his tachyon stashes.

"No!" I yelled.

Professor's body jolted, and he dropped his hands. He stared at me with blank eyes.

My heart pounded at me in a fury for what I'd done. What was wrong with me? Professor didn't deserve to be shouted at. Besides, I couldn't upset him. I needed him to remember his tachyon stashes. The stress was turning me into someone else.

I took a deep breath to bring me back to the Issy I was before all this mess. "I'm sorry, Professor. Who are these cute little girls?"

He hung his head low. A tear slid down the top of his nose and clung to its tip. I immediately wanted to hug him. His sorrow seeped through the ground, right up the soles of my feet. I dreaded that kind of grief. It would be my pain if I couldn't save Mom and Dad.

Rain pattered against the canvas around us as if a hundred rats scurried from the sadness.

Mekasha squeezed Professor's shoulder. "I'm here for ya."

A haze lifted from Professor's eyes. He took the photo from me. "They're my daughters," he choked out. "Sweetest girls."

"Where are they?" I braced myself for an awful answer to match the ache in his voice.

He pressed the frame to his chest. "Lost."

"Lost, where?"

"Lost to the world," he mumbled. "Killed in an automobile accident on Liberty Island."

"There are cars in 1886?" I said. I hadn't seen any on the roads here.

Professor waved me off and whispered, "Not yet." Then

he fell silent.

My chest tightened at the unimaginable sadness of Professor's lost daughters. Mom and Dad always said their world would fall apart if something happened to me. We all might lose each other if Professor couldn't help us. "They are beautiful girls," I said, choking back tears and glancing around the drab tent. No wonder he lived this way. He'd given up.

Mekasha took Professor's hand. "Where is Liberty Island?"

Professor's face took on a hello-are-you-dense stare. "Here in New York," he said. "The island where the Statue of Liberty is."

I whispered to Mekasha, "Isn't it called Bedloe's Island in 1886?" I'd remembered from history class the name didn't change to Liberty Island until the mid-nineteen fifties.

"Yeah, that's it." Mekasha tapped Professor's knee. "Ya mean Bedloe's Island, right, Professor?"

"Liberty Island, boy. Worst day of my life. I never could save them." Professor's eyes watered. "I've learned you can't change history, no matter the number of jumps. Terrible things happen when you try to make big changes. When you tell people things you know will happen to them. Fate is fate." He gave me a haunted frown.

I chewed my bottom lip at Professor's warning. But I had to change history. Just this once to save Mom and Dad.

Professor shook his arms in the air, setting off the chains fringing his jacket sleeves. "What can I help you with, boy? Parts for your projects?"

"Stay with me here, Professor," Mekasha said. "Issy and I are searching for tachyons."

Professor's lips twitched. "White string can make you sing."

I patted Professor's hand. "We'd love your expertise on something."

He straightened, one finger pointed up in the air. "Expertise. Yes, I have some. What would you like to learn? Candy hearts? NECCO candy company makes those. Want to hear about Billy the Kid? Oh, a terrible youth. Delivery boy, too. He would deposit my paper in dog poop. Miss Hopkins never cleaned up after her mutt."

Mekasha's shoulders sunk. "Professor, focus."

"Okay, boy, okay." Professor's eyes came back to the room. "Thinking about tachyons makes my stomach roil, but I can tell they're important to you."

The noxious rat stew stench hit my nose, and I spoke from the corner of my mouth, "That's what turns his belly?"

Mekasha grinned. "Okay, Professor. Issy arrived before her parents. The wormhole opens in a few nights, but we need tachyons to keep it stable. Where'd ya hide yer stashes?"

Professor crossed his arms and gaped beyond us, reciting, "One potato, two potatoes."

"Look at me," Mekasha said to him in a low, steady voice.

"I'm fine. Thinking, boy." He pushed himself up from the chair and circled the tent, stopping to let out an "uh-huh" or scratch an unmentionable spot.

"Is he okay?" I asked Mekasha.

"Yeah. At least he's keeping his trousers hiked up." Mekasha winked.

Professor took four laps around the tent, searing the potato song into my mind. *No bueno.* He fell into his seat and ran his hand through his hair, flattening one side like a matted cat.

"Sorry. I can't remember."

Mekasha's pained expression hit me in the gut. He'd counted on the extra tachyon stashes to rescue his sister. I slumped in my seat, kicking out my foot and catching on Mekasha's satchel. "Wait! Maybe jog his memory with one of his inventions?" I scrabbled through his bag and pulled out the jar.

Professor's eyes lit up. His creation, Luna, held still while I unscrewed the lid. She clicked up the inside wall and balanced at the jar's edge before flitting off. She landed on Professor's shoulder and nestled into his neck.

He leaned his head toward her in devotion. "Luna, you've come home, my sweet daughter."

12 Reunited

MY HEAD SWIVELED to Mekasha. "Daughter?" He twirled his finger around his temple, then pointed to Professor.

Professor held his hand near Luna, and she stepped on, one leg at a time. "Sweet, girl. How are your sisters?"

Sisters?

Luna's wings vibrated in response to Professor.

"Ah, sweetheart. We'll find them," he said.

"Um, Professor? Ya have never called Luna yer daughter."

Professor's finger shot up, an exclamation point in the air. "I remember her now."

"How can a butterfly be your daughter?" I said.

Professor placed Luna on his shoulder. He rubbed his temples. I imagined his memories landing in place, autumn leaves drifting into a pile.

"The butterfly, Luna, was not my daughter when you knew

her," he said to Mekasha. "She transformed into my daughter later, right before I hid her."

Transformed? That was way more exciting than anything I'd written.

Professor pointed to the tallest girl in the photo. "Luna. Thirteen years old at the time." His eyes welled up. "She's my spirited one."

Butterfly Luna raised her forelegs and clicked her wings in response. Professor aimed his finger at the second tallest. "My Star. A dreamer, two years younger than Luna." He sniffled, then hovered his fingers over the third girl, the smallest of the sisters. "Ah, my baby. Seven-year-old Galaxy, the shy one, but always helping others."

The rain picked up, hammering the tarp. A hush fell within the tent. Stillness sucked me in like a vacuum, far away from Mom, Dad, and Aunt Maria. Would I lose them, too?

Mekasha's voice poked a hole in my thought bubble. "Ya named this clockwork butterfly after yer daughter, Luna?"

Professor nodded, and my earlier theory with Mekasha about similar butterflies popped to mind. Professor had three daughters. That meant . . . "Professor, did you make two more butterflies?"

He cocked his head. "Yes, yes. I remember. I named them all after my girls."

Mighty skyscraper! The other two butterflies must've held the tachyon stashes. I caught Mekasha's wink at me. He thought the same. "Professor," I said. "Is this why you consider the butterflies like your daughters? Because of their names?"

He gave his hands a hard clap. "Not *like*. They *are* my daughters."

"I don't get it." Mekasha set a black beetle bug that had crawled up his pant leg on the dirt floor. "How can they be yer daughters?"

Professor leaned into his chair. The rickety seat responded in a creaky fit. "Remarkable, it is. I made the clockworks as a memorial to my daughters. I got Luna to function first but needed more parts for Star and Galaxy."

"Oh, that's why I met only Luna?"

"Exactamundo," Professor said. "You were fond of her and she of you." He chuckled at Luna, who clapped her wings.

Mekasha smiled at her. "The older I got, Luna seemed to become, um." He clicked his tongue. "Smarter."

"You're correct. If you recall, I time jumped right after your tenth birthday. I ended up in the year 2040."

"2040!" Mekasha slapped his knee. "Ya never told me."

"No, no, I didn't. I'd found technology not easily explained. DNA, bringing life to objects."

Mekasha scrunched his face at Professor. "D-N-A?"

Professor stood and clomped out a quick tap dance with his boots, prompting Luna to take flight over to the bookcase. He explained, "Ah yes, DNA. Wonderful little molecules in our bodies." He intertwined his fingers into a pretzel shape. "They form a double helix."

Mekasha clanked together his pocket watches, open-mouthed, eyes glazed. I'd heard about DNA from Mom and Dad, but there were tons of books about it in my time. Here in 1886, I doubted Mekasha learned about it on the streets.

"DNA comes from each of our birth parents," I said. "Like instructions for your body. Tells it how to grow, what to look like."

"Good, Issy," Professor said. "Some people believe DNA influences your character."

Mekasha gave a slow nod. "I get it. What did ya discover in 2040 with DNA?"

Professor peeked outside the tent entrance. Rain poured at the threshold. He tucked the flap tight into its holder then sat in his chair. "You can imagine how advanced the world is in 2040. I won't spoil the surprises for you, Issy." He snickered, wiggling his fingers in the air. "Let's say there won't be a need for laptops. Everything at your tips."

I could only imagine what he knew. I laughed and wiggled my digits back at him.

"I met a scientist who dabbled in animal DNA," Professor continued. "He used it to re-animate the personality of a dead cat into a stuffed animal."

"Hold up." I had something important to say. "That's gross."

"It's unique," Professor said. "No doubt, there were issues with the technology, but the scientist gave me enough information to come up with a method in 1886. It's much better if you ask me."

"What are ya saying, Professor?"

"I returned to our time and worked on my version of re-animation, giving Luna her advanced thought process."

Mekasha's face went blank. "She can think? Whose DNA did ya use for her?"

I wanted to shake him, but instead, I pointed to the photo of Professor's daughters with the best "duh" face I could muster from behind my mask.

Mekasha paused. "Oh! Luna yer *human* daughter," he said.

Professor took off his hat. He hugged it while he rose from

the chair and wandered over to butterfly Luna, extending his hand. She climbed onto his palm. "Yes, my daughter Luna's DNA, reanimated in a clockwork butterfly." His eyes moistened.

"Professor, could ya make one of Naya?" Mekasha's face held so much hope.

"Oh, oh." Professor's mouth turned down. Rain dropped heavy on the tent top like drum beats. "Boy, this world took my daughters, but Naya is still out there. You will find her."

A thread of Mekasha's fun personality unraveled, and his shoulders sunk along with my heart. I wished I could take away his pain.

Luna flitted over to Mekasha's hand and pranced in his palm. He bowed his head to her. "Yeah, girl, I still have ya."

"Professor, how'd you have DNA from your daughter since she—" I couldn't bring myself to finish the thought.

Professor shuffled over to a wicker basket and flung off its cover. He raised his arms and dipped his hands inside, then swooped them up, a small chest in hand. He sure had a thing for flair. "My most treasured possession."

He brought it into the light, a rectangular pink case the size of a small shoebox. He propped open the lid. A miniature model of the solar system flipped up from the center and spun to clinky music. Those types of jewelry cases usually had a ballerina inside. I'd no idea they existed in the 1800s.

"Our lovely-locks box of first haircuts." Professor tapped his finger along three tiny jars inside, each holding a bundle of strawberry-tinted strands. "I saved it from the fire."

"Ya never spoke of a fire," Mekasha said.

"Not the most fun story." Professor's face darkened. "A fire ravaged our home not long after the girls perished in the car accident. Their mother, my wife Lilian, couldn't handle losing our precious daughters. She set the house ablaze and ran away."

An ache crept behind my naval. How much could a person handle? My parents moving me to Cornville and banning me from their lab didn't seem so bad now. I removed my mask—no sense hiding my face. I needed to be myself right now. That was how I'd help Professor.

Cue the rain. It had a mind of its own, pummeling the tent like horse hooves. The lantern light flickered.

"Ah, there she is." Professor nodded at me. "Pretty as ever."

My face warmed. "You've never seen me without the mask, Professor. How would you know I'm pretty as ever?"

"Because the pretty on your inside matches the pretty on your outside," he said.

My breath caught. Mom would've said something like that.

"Let's see if I can remember where I hid the other two tachyon stashes." Professor sat and observed me. "You found Luna at your house."

"Wait, how'd you know that?" I said. "We didn't tell you where Luna came from."

Professor twiddled his fingers. "Well, I just assumed. No matter, I'm glad you have her."

"Do ya think tachyons are inside the clockwork butterflies for Star and Galaxy?"

"Ah, maybe, boy." Professor rubbed his nose. "I was in a panic for some reason. Had to place them fast. Something about getting ahead."

"Maybe ya were trying to get ahead of Boss finding yer

tachyons?"

Professor snapped his fingers. "Dal, Chal, Clunk, what were their names?"

"Sal and Chunk!" I shouted.

"Yes, you got it." Professor jiggled his finger in his ear.

"Sorry for yelling," I said. His excitement had caught me up.

"Quite all right, Issy. Sometimes I find it fun to yell at random moments." He waggled his brows.

A gust of wind blew the tent flap open, and rain whipped inside. Mekasha jumped up to secure the entrance. Lightning hit the ground outside. Screams chimed from folks determined to remain at the bazaar.

"Whoa, too close." My stomach roiled, and the air wavered before my eyes. I snuggled against Dad's backpack, trying to stop the nausea.

"Okay, Professor. Sal and Chunk were coming for yer tachy—"

CRACK!

We all flinched at another lightning strike. Outside, it lit like daylight for two full seconds. Thunder boomed. Had Whiz followed me to the past?

"Away from the door, boy!" Professor waved Mekasha over and gave a curious scowl at the weather. "Something is in the air."

ZAP!

Electricity blistered the tent. I screamed and threw myself to the ground.

"Issy, where are ya?" Mekasha yelled over the snaps and pops.

"I'm here. I'm okay. Where's Professor?"

"Issy!" A voice, not Professor's, not Mekasha's, rang out.

Smoke filled my eyes and mouth. I coughed, straining to hear.

"Isadora!"

The roar in my ears quieted as the haze in the tent faded. I peered around, and my eyes spotted a full-figured body. "Aunt Maria?"

13 Galaxy

I PUSHED MYSELF up to my knees and rubbed my eyes. My head throbbed with each thunder of my pulse.

"*Mija.*"

My eyes widened. "Aunt Maria, you're here!" She helped me to my feet and swept me into a bear hug. I was so happy she found a way to get to me.

"*Sí, sí.*" She held me at arm's length. Her pizza-wide smile displayed her relief. "And we'll talk about your outfit later," she whispered, wagging her finger up and down my clothes with enough gusto it was clear she had no aches from her time jump.

The pounding in my skull slowed, and I glanced around the tent. No damage from the lightning, the same as what happened at home. How had Aunt Maria opened a wormhole and landed exactly where I was?

Mekasha gave my *tía* a polite nod then sidled over to me.

"Professor is out cold."

The red-headed genius lay sprawled by the bookcase, thrown clear from his chair. Luna flitted to his forehead while I crouched at his side.

"Professor, wake up." I pushed on his shoulder. "Wake up."

Mekasha placed two fingers against Professor's neck. "His pulse is strong."

Aunt Maria eased herself down, one knee at a time. Luna clacked her wings and raised her front legs. "Oh, you, *mariposa*."

"Her name is Luna," I said.

"Whatever it is. She's in my way." Aunt Maria shooed Luna and pulled on Professor's chin, then placed her ear above his open mouth. "He's breathing." She closed his mouth and pinched his nose. "A quick squeeze should do it."

Professor's eyes flew open. He swatted at Aunt Maria's arm, sending her to her rump. "*Aye-yai-yai*, that hurt." She gathered her skirt, primped her hair with two quick hand swishes, then shoved herself to a stand.

"Wh-what happened?" Professor sat up and belched. He waved his hand over his mouth. "Excuse me. I haven't had a drink, but it sure feels like I have."

Mekasha held two fingers in front of Professor's face. "How many do ya see?"

"Boy, I'm fine."

"What's the last thing you remember?" I said.

He stood one wobbly appendage at a time, like a newborn ostrich gaining its footing. "I told Mekasha to stay away from the door and—" His eyes widened at Aunt Maria.

"*¿Qué?*" She elbowed me. "What's he looking at?"

Professor moved near her. "You came through a wormhole. You must have tachyons."

Of course! Aunt Maria found more tachyons. Warmth spread throughout my chest, radiating up my neck into the biggest chipmunk smile. Mekasha would have a vessel now to find his sister. And I could use Luna. But then my grin fell. With Aunt Maria here, I doubted Luna had enough strength to get my entire family home.

Mekasha's excitement wasn't quite there. His eyes bored into Aunt Maria. "Where are the tachyons? I have to have them."

Aunt Maria clutched her purse, glaring from Mekasha to Professor. "*¡Para el carro!*" Her thick Spanish accent gave a punch to the "hold your horses" statement.

"*La calma abajo, por favor,*" Professor said.

I did a double-take. Professor, Spanish?

"Calm down? You don't know me to tell me to calm down." Aunt Maria swayed her head with the rhythm of each word. "Can you tell me where to find my brother and his wife?" She raised her painted brows. Professor gave her a blank stare. "No?" she said. "Then we leave."

"*Tía,* it's okay." I rested my hand on her arm. "They're my friends." The word rolled off my tongue, tingling my insides. Luna clanked from her spot on the bookcase. "Luna, too."

Aunt Maria's head retreated like a turtle in its shell. Her double jowl turned to three. "Your *amigos?* Eh, Issy, *mija.*" She gave Mekasha and Professor another once over.

Professor motioned to his armchair. "Please, Lady Maria, have a seat."

She eyed him. "Fine, but no funny business."

I returned to my chair and Mekasha to his. He kept a watchful eye on my *tía's* purse as Professor dragged over a box to close the circle. He sat on it beside Aunt Maria.

She hugged her purse to her chest. "You look like a bunch of tarsiers, sitting there, staring at me."

I laughed at the image of the Yoda-like monkeys she'd called them. "*Tía,* how'd you find me? Where did you get tachyons?"

"*Sí,* I will tell you, but my head hurts." She rubbed her forehead.

"Brain scramble," Mekasha said all casual as if saying, "fine day, don't ya think?"

I kicked out my boot. A few inches closer, I could've notched him in the shin. He mouthed, "Sorry."

"What is brain scramble?" Aunt Maria hunted our faces for an answer.

Professor waved his arm in a grand gesture. "So horrid. I have it."

"Have what?" Aunt Maria tugged my hand. "Issy, we're going. I don't like all this talk about brain-whatever. We need to find your parents."

"Please, we'll explain. He makes it sound worse than it is. One jump won't hurt us." I threw a couple of eye-darts at Professor, and he clammed up. "Mekasha can describe it better."

She considered me a moment. "Fine, a few minutes." She slid the purse within her skirt folds and pursed her lips at Mekasha. "*Sí,* smart boy, let's hear it."

"It's like this." He put on the charm as he explained, showcasing his upper row of teeth (plus the gap).

Aunt Maria's head retreated again, her triple chin in full

force. "Issy and I are okay since we jumped only one time?"

"*Sí, Tía.* We're fine."

"*Ahora,* but what about the trip home?"

"My special liquid." Mekasha tapped the vials on his breast pocket. "An herbal blend to enhance the brain's ability to recover."

"Why didn't Professor use it?" Aunt Maria eyed the genius.

"Because he wouldn't wait for me to complete the recipe." Mekasha wagged his finger at him.

"Guilty." Professor stuck out his wrists in a handcuffed position. "The boy is smart," he said. "I knew he'd come up with something, but in the meantime, I had to keep jumping. To find the parts to give Luna and her sisters their personalities."

At hearing her name, Luna flitted to Professor's shoulder and pranced in a circle.

"She's a metal insect," Aunt Maria said. She threw her hands up, rattling her bracelets. "How much personality can she have?"

Luna flew, circling Aunt Maria's head and popping off a gear.

"Enough to know she doesn't like you," Professor said with a smile.

"*Ahora,* I've had *enough.*" Aunt Maria pushed herself up. "*Mija,* let's go. It's weird here. Brain scramble, a junk-yard *mariposa,* and what's with the clothes?"

Mekasha reached for Aunt Maria's purse. "I need those tachyons."

"*No bueno.*" She snatched her bag to her side and said to Issy, "I found those tacky things you talked about, at least I think I did. These are for us." She faced Mekasha and tossed her chin toward Luna. "Use *that* butterfly."

"No!" Professor shielded Luna with his hand. "You can't

take her. She's jumped too many times."

Aunt Maria and Professor bickered while Mekasha went stone silent. His eyes darkened with the lantern flame flickering against his pupils. He edged over to the bookcase, trailing his hand along the shelf, before bringing up his fist and slamming it down.

"I *will* have tachyons!"

Silence engulfed the tent. Now, Aunt Maria resembled a tarsier monkey while Professor poked a finger in his ear.

"Mekasha, you're right," I said in a hushed voice. "You'll get the tachyons." I shook my head at the supposed adults around me. "Professor, you miss your daughters. Luna is the closest you've got to having your daughter back, but Mekasha's sister is alive and needs him." Then to my *tía*, "And you of all people understand how important family is. We help Mekasha and Professor first. I owe them, especially Mekasha."

Aunt Maria relaxed her face and took her seat again. She clasped my hands. "You have a kind heart, *mija*." She turned to Professor and Mekasha. "We will help."

My heart swelled with love for her.

Mekasha paced the tent, scuffing his boots along the ground and fiddling with his pocket watches. "Thank you. Sorry for my outburst. I just can't shake that I may never see Naya again." His face reflected deep thought. After the fifth turnabout, he stopped and clicked his heels together. "We shouldn't take Luna from Professor."

"Why can't you return her to him after finding your sister?" Aunt Maria said.

"Like I told Issy, tachyons don't provide endless energy for jumps." Mekasha watched Professor's face.

Professor winced then touched Luna's wing. "Once the energy is used up, the vessel is destroyed."

I gasped. I knew a vessel could only handle so many jumps. But destroyed afterward? No wonder Professor protected Luna so fiercely. He could lose her forever. "How many more jumps does she have?"

"Don't know." Professor tossed his hand. "She jumped quite a bit with me in the past."

My head swam. Luna wouldn't be enough for my whole family. I'd need the tachyon source in Aunt Maria's purse, which meant we must find Professor's other two stashes. One more for me and one for Mekasha.

"*Tía*, what's the tachyon vessel you found at home?"

Aunt Maria held her purse close. "I was only going to show it to you, *mija*, but in light of what's going on." She dipped her chin toward Professor and opened her bag to reveal a glass jar.

"Galaxy!" Professor inched forward, taking the jar into his palms. "My baby girl."

14 Who Knows

ANOTHER CLOCKWORK BUTTERFLY twitched its wings and clanked its legs from inside the glass jar. Swirling gold wire adorned her wings like the endless whirls of the Milky Way. Professor removed the lid, freeing Galaxy. She circled above, and Luna flitted up to join her. The sisters flew a figure-eight over his head, their gears in joyous spins. They landed on Professor's shoulder with Galaxy snuggling into her big sister, Luna.

"Where'd you find her, *Tia?*"

Aunt Maria shifted in her seat. "After you disappeared, Issy, I lost it, went *loco*. Even the Saints couldn't rid my tears." She spun a curl of her hair around her finger. "The storm moved on, but that shimmery hole you'd disappeared into stayed open."

"Wait, the wormhole didn't close after Issy's jump?" Professor flicked his ear. "They usually dissipate quickly without sustained tachyon energy." He studied my face, one brow upright. "There must be a much larger source at your home to have opened the hole *and* kept it viable. Interesting, indeed."

I shrugged. "Maybe inside my parents' lab? We didn't have time to look through all of it."

"Anyway," Aunt Maria huffed, shifting our attention back to her again. "I knew I had to go after you, *mija,* but I remembered a wormhole would collapse without tachyons. I put two-and-two together with that mechanical butterfly and the wormhole. I went searching the barn, and the wardrobe mirror flashed again."

My eyes widened. "What did you see?"

"A butterfly. Inside the glass."

"I saw it in the lab, too." My excitement bubbled.

Mekasha sat on the chair's edge. "How'd ya get her out?"

"Luna's puzzle box," Aunt Maria said.

Mekasha crumpled his forehead. "But the butterfly be inside the mirror, not the box."

"Right." Aunt Maria bent over, picked up an imaginary object, and heaved it. "I smashed the mirror. Like *Super Muñeco* would." She brought up her elbow then crushed it down into the palm of her other hand. Just like the *Lucha Libre* wrestling she watched all the time.

"Brilliant." I laughed.

She fluffed her hair and pursed her lips. "*Sí.* I got a few of those Garcia smarts. The butterfly escaped and hid behind beakers. I couldn't coax her out. She's timid, unlike her lively sister."

Professor reached his finger near his neck, under Galaxy's feet. She backed away. Luna nudged her a bit, and Galaxy padded onto Professor's hand. He held her up. "Youngest of

the sisters. She's always in their shadows."

Aunt Maria shrugged. "I threw a cloth on her, put her into a jar, and ran to the family room. Lightning struck, then poof . . ." she flung out her fingers, "I was here."

"So little Galaxy has enough tachyon strength for jumps?" Mekasha said, his cheeks rising with his eyebrows.

"Why, yes, yes." Professor waggled a finger. "I never jumped with Galaxy. She'll be plenty for your family, Issy."

Mekasha's smile faded at the mention of my family, but my eyes sprung wide. "I can take her?"

Galaxy clinked her antennae in a cheery chime.

"Yes, she's ready to step out from her sisters," Professor said. "Luna will remain with me."

Mekasha's eyes fell, his shoulders slumped, and he remained quiet.

"Professor, where's Star?" We had to reunite the last sister and get a tachyon source for Mekasha.

He rubbed his forehead. "I wish I knew, but my brain hurts. It's close to midnight. Maybe some sleep will help me think clearer tomorrow?"

"Yeah, Professor. Ya need rest." Mekasha's pained gaze at him stung my heart. I shouldn't push Professor too hard.

"You're right, let's rest on it," I said with as much chirpiness as I could muster.

Mekasha pulled straw mats and blankets from a corner, giving glances at Professor, whose face sagged with his labored steps. Going through the painful memories of his daughters had taken a toll on the red-haired genius. We set up beds on the floor, Aunt Maria with me on one side of the tent, the boys on the other.

A soft rain pattered the canvas top. I snuggled into my *tía* and willed my mind not to ponder the rats who didn't make it into Professor's stew. Professor dimmed the lantern to a firefly's glow. He relaxed in his chair, chattering to his daughters. The odd family reunion gave me a sense of hope that I'd be with Mom and Dad soon. My eyelids drooped into sleep.

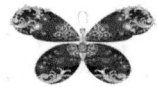

NEXT MORNING, I woke to a familiar sweet aroma. *Pan dulce*. Oh yeah. I stretched and rubbed the gunk from my eyes. The lantern still offered a warm glow around the tent. Aunt Maria perched herself on a short stool near the brick oven. She kneaded dough on a wooden plank, sprinkling in sugar with each fold.

"*Buenos días, mija.*" She grinned. "Sleep okay?"

"Yeah." I scanned the empty beds. "Where're Mekasha and Professor?"

"They left for water and meats. I found a crate here with flour and sugar to at least make you warm bread." She pointed to a pile of steaming rolls.

"Umm, *Tía*, where'd you find eggs for the dough?"

"You wouldn't believe. I heard a *cluck-cluck* here, a *cluck-cluck* there. Stuck my head out the tent door. A chicken stopped right outside on a hay pile. Left me an egg."

I laughed the belly-shaking kind and gave her a suspicious eye. "Are you serious?"

"*Sí*, I'm not joking." She joined me in laughing and doubled over, then slapped her knee and took a deep breath, chuckling one more time.

"That's what I call home delivery." I lugged myself happily over for a roll. Mom taught me how to make *pan dulce* years ago. We used all sorts of colored sugar for the toppings. I savored the first bite, aching to have breakfast with my parents.

Mekasha and Professor barged into the tent, and Mekasha raised a fat sausage tied to a rope. "A little pork for yer fork?" He handed it to Aunt Maria.

"Tempting." I scrunched my nose at the meat, then checked out Professor in his pants, jacket, and burgundy bowler hat covered in gears and chains. "You look rested, Professor." His eyes still drooped, but there was a liveliness in them.

He removed his hat and bowed. "Yes, a splendid day. The girls joined us. Off you go, sweethearts." Luna and Galaxy flitted from his arm to the bookcase. He rubbed his forehead several times.

"You okay, Professor?" I said.

Mekasha frowned, his eyes full of concern. Was the brain scramble worse?

"Oh, a little headache. No big deal." Professor shuffled over to Aunt Maria and patted her shoulder. "Whatever you've made, it smells wonderful."

She smiled up at him. "Breakfast is served." She handed out battered tin plates piled with sweet bread.

Professor took a bite and winked at her. "Ah, this bread is sweet like the loving hands that made it."

I jerked up my eyes. Aunt Maria's reaction would be epic. She'd taken me to a fish market once, and a man called her "sweet." She smacked him upside the head with the tail end of a sockeye salmon, a few choice words included.

To my surprise, Aunt Maria blushed and batted her eyelashes like a fluttering butterfly. At Professor? What happened to her gruffness toward him last night? A few nice words had done the trick.

We ate in comfortable silence—the warm, fuzzy family kind.

Professor eyed Aunt Maria, and she lowered her eyes with a giggle. Seriously, what was going on with those two? I ate the last of my food and wiped my hands on a cloth. "Professor," I said, "any luck remembering where Star is?"

He picked at his teeth with a twig. "No, nope. Only remembered I had to get ahead on the trek to Liberty Island."

"Ahead to Liberty Island, ya say?" Mekasha clicked his tongue.

"Yes, such a tragic place. Where my daughters—" He lowered his head.

Poor Professor. His mind jumped from now to whatever point in the future his daughters' fatal car accident had taken place.

Aunt Maria patted Professor's knee. "A beautiful island for a lovely statue."

Professor set his plate aside and stood. "Did you know the statue arrived in pieces? I saw a head, sitting there, all by itself."

"A head?" Aunt Maria laughed. "Must've been a sight."

I gawked at Professor. "A head?"

"Why yes," he said. "They displayed the statue's head, not too far from here, before they attached it to the body."

I gasped, then turned to Mekasha. "You catch that? 'A head.' Remember Professor said he needed to get ahead to the island?"

Mekasha dropped his bread roll. "Professor had to get *a* head. Not *ahead* of Boss but a *head*. A place to stash the tachyons."

I jumped up. "Professor! You hid the third butterfly in the Statue of Liberty's head."

Professor's eyes took on several shapes. Wide, narrow, crossed. "Hmm, possible." He tugged on his hair, muttering, "Hide. A. Head." Then snapped his fingers. "I got it. I hid Star in the statue's head."

"Yes, you did." I gave a thumb-up to Aunt Maria and Mekasha. They returned the gesture and smiled at Professor.

"How do we get inside the head?" Aunt Maria said.

Mekasha smoothed the sleeves of his leather jacket and winked. "Leave it to me. I'll get us there. But, one problem. We need to know the statue's entrance beforehand, so we can enter fast and not risk being seen by soldiers patrolling the waters."

How would we locate a spot to enter? The statue was huge. My mind spun, crisscrossing through my story. Jocko's investigation led to the Statue of Liberty, but he hadn't gone inside. *Although!*

My eyes lit up. "The main character in my book had to keep the statue's design a secret by hiding its blueprints."

"Where'd he hide them?" Aunt Maria twisted the bangles on her wrist.

"New York City Hall," I said.

"Issy, if the blueprints are part of yer story, wouldn't the statue's design be in yer head?"

My cheeks heated. It was a plot hole that I needed to fix. "Well, I skipped that part. Jocko does protect the blueprints, but I never created the design to show the reader. I don't know the statue's layout."

Mekasha's eyes brightened. "If Jocko hid the blueprints in yer book, then it's good enough for me. We head to City Hall."

"I'll accompany you," Professor said, his eyes glazing over.

"Professor, ya stay here." Mekasha guided him back to his chair. "We need ya to hold down the fort."

"Well, okay, boy." Professor's smile at Mekasha was full of trust.

Aunt Maria gathered up her skirt. "Then I'll go with you."

"Oh, no, you don't, *Tía*. There'll be guards if City Hall is even a little like my book. We'll need to be fast. I can't have you taken away from me, too." My eyes skittered to Professor. He was breathing hard and rubbing a wet cloth over his head. "We need you *here*."

Aunt Maria grumbled, but her eyes softened as she watched Professor. "Okay, *mija*. I'll cover things here. You got this." She patted Professor's hand. "We both know you got this."

Professor nodded. "Yes, yes, of course."

Mekasha came to my side and squeezed my hand. "Thanks."

I squeezed back. Aunt Maria would take good care of Professor.

The plan was set. We'd sneak into City Hall that evening for the blueprints. We spent the next six hours cleaning and stocking food for Professor. Countdown to *Operation Liberty Head*.

Mekasha took us to the bazaar's wardrobe tents for new outfits in the afternoon. Aunt Maria settled on a long blue skirt, short-heeled black boots, with a black, ruffled long-sleeved blouse. I kept my leather jacket, rust-colored pants, and boots but replaced the black corset and white shirt with a mahogany-colored, short-sleeved top, ruffled up the front and around my neck.

Mekasha bargained (more like charmed) with the merchant,

who agreed to four glass marbles. She must've thought she scored the big one. Mekasha could weave a believable backstory on the previous marble owners. Today, it was Emily Dickinson's rare orbs he used for payment.

WE ARRIVED BACK at Professor's tent to find him bent over the stew pot.

"What'd ya make for dinner?" Mekasha sniffed the air.

Professor replaced the lid, smacking his lips. "I couldn't trap another rat, pesky things, so tonight is beef."

"I bet it'll be *bueno*." Aunt Maria nudged Professor with her hip. He responded with a delightful clap. "I'll whip up a batch of handmade corn tortillas," she said.

Dinner proved another comfortable meal. Aunt Maria sat near Professor and taught him to use a tortilla to grab the meat from his tin bowl and make a mini taco.

"Professor," I said. "Where in the head did you hide Star?"

He tapped his fork to his ear. "Been thinking about that. Then it hit me. I'd written a clue." He took a paper from his jacket pocket. "Found it in the girls' lovely-locks box. It reads: Who knows? Do I knows? Do you knows? Who could possibly knows?" He folded the note and went back to eating.

I threw my hands up and huffed, "What does *that* mean?"

Professor flicked his nose with a shrug, and my hope of a successful mission faded.

With such a vague clue, our chances of finding Star inside

the massive statue's head were about the same as me running faster than the speed of light.

15 Toboggan Run

MEKASHA REPEATED THE clue aloud for us. The phrase didn't make sense to me, but Professor's words usually had a double meaning. "Maybe you told someone where you hid Star. Is the clue to remind you that someone *else* knows where she is?"

Professor stopped mid-chew. His left cheek bulged like a hamster storing food. "Nope, I wouldn't have told anyone. No one to trust." He hiccupped and nodded at Mekasha. "Except you, boy, but I didn't want to put you in danger. Boss would've taken you."

I played the words over in my head. *Knows, knows, knows.* Wait. "Nose!" I shouted excitedly.

"*Mija*, stop yelling." Aunt Maria covered her ears.

"Sorry, it's—"

"Yes, that must be it." Mekasha patted my shoulder. "Ya figured it out, Issy."

"*¿Qué?*" Aunt Maria said. "Figured out what?"

I pointed to my sniffer. "Professor hid Star in the Statue of Liberty's *nose.*"

"Why, yes, yes!" Professor stood, breaking into a jig dance. He held out his hand to Aunt Maria. Her face flushed with a playful smile, and she rose. He spun her around the tent while Mekasha stomped out a beat for them.

Aunt Maria fell into her chair, fanning herself with a rag. "*Oye!* I haven't danced in years. *Gracias.*" She blew Professor a kiss. He caught it with his hand and placed it into his breast pocket. My *tía's* maple flan dessert couldn't beat the sappiness in this tent.

"Now we *knows,* so let's get to work," I said.

We finished dinner, then Mekasha and I prepared to leave for City Hall to search for the blueprints. We'd have a better chance after City Hall closed and the workers went home. I put on my mask for disguise. It made our caper much more exciting. Mekasha shoved on his hat and goggles. He stocked his pouch with glass and magnetic marbles.

"Ya up for the plan, Issy?" Mekasha attached his slingshot to his belt.

"Does the earth do a full rotation every 23 hours, 56 minutes, and 4 seconds, give or take?" I teased and wiggled into my backpack. Of course, I was up for *Operation Liberty Head.* My parents' lives depended on it. "Why do you ask?"

He clicked his tongue. "I have an interesting way to travel there."

A few days ago, no way I'd have followed anyone on a wild quest. I would've left Mekasha, done it myself. But now, I knew while maybe I could have saved my parents alone, it was much better with him. Is this what Mom meant by finding my tribe? "All right, let's go."

His tooth-gapped grin took over his face, and he headed for the door.

I hugged Aunt Maria. "*Adiós.* See you soon."

"Be safe." She choked on her words. "Watch for those guards."

"Keep the *pan dulce* warm for us." I kissed her cheek and left the tent with Mekasha.

We exited the Bizarre Bazaar under a half-lit first-quarter moon. It wouldn't be long until waxing gibbous—the time my parents arrived. The time I had to be on that dock for them.

Our trek over the fields and to the outskirts of New York City allowed my thoughts to run amuck. How would we sneak into City Hall? What if I was wrong and we didn't find the statue's blueprints there? Or the blueprints were blank?

Mekasha rattled through my despair with talk about how Naya loved to read novels. I wondered what type of stories she liked. Fantasy? Romance? Sci-Fi? He suggested I give her a copy of my book when I came back to visit. I laughed it off. After seeing this world, my book didn't do it justice. I wouldn't want anyone from here reading it.

"Issy, I bet yer book is great. I never met anyone who could write a story about a place they'd never been to."

"Good point." But the thought itched at my brain. How could I have made up an entire place that already existed? I mean, Mekasha, Professor, the butterflies . . . they were real. They've always been here, right? The complicated equation was worse than when Mom explained Albert Einstein's theory of gravity.

Who would've thought that gravity is technically not a force? My current situation was too much to calculate, so I flipped the conversation. "How do we get into City Hall?"

"Underground." Mekasha tipped his hat.

"Ewww, like in the sewers?"

"No, the control room in the abandoned subway station underneath City Hall."

I gave him a sideways glance. "You can get us through there?"

"I have my ways." He winked in his exaggerated Mekasha style.

"How did you learn so much about City Hall?"

His face took on the look of a young kid whose top scoop from his ice cream cone had toppled to the ground. "My dad used to work in City Hall. He met Mom there as a teenager. Naya and I would ride the subway with our grandmother to pick them up."

"Did you ever go inside City Hall?" I tried to keep his mind off his parents. I knew what it was like to miss a mom and dad.

"Yeah, I'd use the abandoned subway to sneak into City Hall. A way to feel close to my family. The best part is dodging the security guards." His face lit up, erasing all sadness as we trudged on.

We arrived near the Brooklyn Bridge. Massive gears rotated along its sides, powering the lights strung along the entire length.

"This beauty was built three years ago." Mekasha gazed up at the structure then grabbed my arm. "Get down!"

"What's wrong?" I huddled behind a bush with him.

"Remember when I told ya Boss is a Time Pirate?" He pointed upward.

I drew my eyes to the hovering pirate ship. Steam sprayed from its back end while shafts and gears cranked hard. Jump'n enchilada! It was the same flying vessel from the night I met Mekasha. I half expected a rope to come barreling over the ship's side with a pirate monkey scurrying down to investigate us. Instead, after a few moments, the boat spewed a ball of steam and drifted away.

Mekasha watched to be sure they'd gone. "Boss lives on it. Only a few of Boss's lackeys are allowed on the ship. I've seen it docked in a field near Bizarre Bazaar before. Boss must be patrolling for tachyons tonight. We better go."

We left for City Hall Park. Few people walked the paths as street vendors packed up shop, wheeling away steam-powered machines for sausages and coffee. A man skirted by us with two automaton dogs on leashes, their metal teeth gnashing at me. I flung myself out of their way.

Mekasha ran to me. "Ya, okay?"

I couldn't catch my breath. "I, I don't have those in my book."

"It's okay, Issy. I got ya." He stared into my eyes, leading me to the path.

I calmed with each step, Mekasha by my side, and we hit a new road. Steam-powered street lamps lined the trail, spitting water at us on the way by. Mekasha stopped at a utility hole in the ground.

I crossed my arms. "I thought you said no sewer."

"No sewer." He lugged off the cover with a grunt and stepped down through the hole onto a wall ladder. "A quick ride. I won't let ya get hurt."

Without hesitation, I followed him. Such an odd sensation

to have complete trust in someone.

We descended the ladder onto the concrete floor of a dark cavern. Mekasha rummaged through his satchel. "Darn. I forgot my torch."

"Wait, I have one." I pulled a metal cylinder the size of a flashlight from my backpack. "You got a match?"

"I do." He leaned in and ran his ringers over the cylinder. "Ya made this?"

"Yep. Jocko uses one in my story." I removed a domed glass cover from one end, revealing a stiff cotton string soaked in oil. It stuck out from the center of a small circular mirror. "Light it here."

Mekasha struck the match on his vest and lit the wick. I replaced the dome. Light flooded from the glass. He smiled. "It's bright."

"The reflections from the mirror bounce the light waves off the surfaces then out the glass top. These tiny holes along the side of the cylinder allow the air to vent, so the flame stays lit."

I handed the gadget to him, and he aimed it into the dark tunnel. Light blazed across the smooth metal walls and into a shaft descending at a slight angle like a water park slide.

"These tunnels are the old City Hall Post Office delivery routes. Mail used to travel around the city, underneath the streets. But now, mail sorting is done by humanoid automatons, and armored mechanical pigeons drop the parcels at folk's front doors."

"We'll be putting these tunnels back into use?" I arched my brow at him.

He laughed. "Ya got it."

I stepped one foot inside the tube, but Mekasha seized my arm.

"No, Issy. The metal be too smooth. Ya would slip. Shoot straight off before I could catch ya."

Shivers skipped across my arms at the thought of sliding into oblivion. "Now what?"

Mekasha reached above the tunnel entrance and cranked a handle. A clatter erupted from inside the opening as a metal sheet on the sidewall slipped upward into the curved ceiling. Steam poured from the cavity, and a platform holding a toboggan slid out.

My legs wobbled. This wasn't a slow-snow-toboggan. It was like the kind used in the Winter Olympics. The fast ones. "Our ride?"

Mekasha grinned wider than the tunnel. "Hop in."

I hesitated, then stepped inside the brass bullet and settled into the rear leather seat, cracked and faded from years of use. Mekasha swiped a match and reached out to the sled's nose, igniting several wicks behind a large glass plate. Light burst forth, brighter than my flashlight gadget, now blown out and tucked away in my backpack. I peeked over his shoulder at the controls and stiffened. No steering wheel. "How do you drive?"

He planted himself in the front chair, pulling several levers on a switch panel. "About that. The steering is disabled in all these mail movers. But I can trigger the backup sensors to change course."

"Ch-change course?" I gripped the sides of the toboggan.

Mekasha chuckled. "Issy, I won't allow a scratch to ya head. Buckle up."

147

I released my white-knuckled grip and fumbled around my seat. My hands found heavy leather straps bolted to either side. I wrapped them around my waist with a hard shove to join the buckles, then I took off my mask. This was a good time for my goggles.

"Here we go." Mekasha cranked a dial on the control panel. The platform tipped forward to a stop. I leaned back to stay upright while Mekasha flipped three switches. A fog rose from the tunnel floor.

"Total tamales, what's happening?" I wiped mist from my lenses.

"Steam builds in a channel underneath the tunnels. The pressure will burst from hundreds of holes in the floor to keep the mail carrier afloat."

In seconds, steam spewed short blasts of air in close intervals. Mekasha jabbed a gold button, sending the toboggan off the platform. Steam caught the vehicle, and we hovered a few inches off the ground. We bobbed around until Mekasha slammed his palm on a large knob, discharging vapor from the toboggan's end. We zoomed forward and jetted headlong, my hair whipping back in a lion's mane.

Up ahead, the tunnel branched into two directions. Mekasha toyed with his slingshot as if he were a casual observer on a train at the zoo. We neared the intersection, but the mail carrier didn't slow, and Mekasha didn't react.

My scalp tightened, certain we'd crash this death bullet. "We'll hit the divider!"

He patted my hand then steadied himself with his foot wedged into a crevice. He brought up his slingshot at the last

possible moment, aimed, and let a marble fly. The little sphere collided with a geared contraption in the upper-right ceiling. The steam in the floor shifted, causing the toboggan to tilt a smidge then continue into the right-hand side of the intersection.

My balled-up anxiety spouted into laughter. "Are you kidding me?!"

Mekasha turned with his tooth-gapped grin and signature wink. He continued "steering" with his perfect aim, and we sped underneath the streets of New York City.

16 Mr. Automaton

IN NO TIME, we arrived at an abandoned wooden dock underneath City Hall, our only light coming from the toboggan's headlamp. Mekasha pressed a few pedals, slowing us to a stop next to a platform with a sign that read: *Mail Station*.

I unbuckled and hopped from the mail carrier, pushing up the goggles and securing my mask back in place. I shivered at the shadows playing in every corner and the scampering of rodent feet. Stale, damp air squelched my breathing, but my relit flashlight burned bright. Since oxygen feeds fire, I knew there was plenty of good air.

"Over here." Mekasha waved me to a ladder attached to a brick wall covered in cobwebs and moss. He climbed the first few rungs and called over his shoulder, "Leads to the old mailroom in City Hall. Only room no longer used in the building."

I stuck my flashlight inside my pack with the lit end sticking out, then followed him up, gripping the steel rails. Rust-covered rungs squeaked against the old bolts anchored into the wall. "Are we c-close?" We'd gone higher than the shelf ladder in my parents' lab.

"Ya doing great, Issy. Another foot or so."

I pressed on until Mekasha stopped to push open a trap door. Its splintered planks and hinges screamed of abandonment. Good thing no one was around to hear its protests. I handed over the flashlight, and he crawled through. "All clear," he called down.

Two more steps and I scuttled up to my knees onto a concrete floor littered with letter waste. Six-foot-tall mail sorter cases surrounded us, their empty cavities begging for new envelopes. We clomped by in silence toward the exit door.

Mekasha paused mid-step and held up his hand. "Ya hear that?"

"No, what?" My eyes strained in the dim light. We stepped a few paces. A light *tap tap* followed. "I heard *that*."

We moved again, and the *tap-tap-tap* echoed in unison with our stride. Our steps echoed faster. The *tap-tap-tap* sped up.

Mekasha stiffened. He grabbed my hand and bolted. "Watch out—" He skidded sideways, pulling me to my bottom. I spotted the source of the *tap-tap* and scooched back faster than a crab running from a seagull.

¿En serio? A copper mechanical man marched to a nearby mail sorter case. He stopped, eyes glued on us.

"An automaton." Mekasha helped me inch up then placed himself in front of me.

I gazed around his top hat. The automaton's dented metal head tilted like a curious puppy. Battered brass lids hovered over

hollowed eyes. They shuddered down and up in one sluggity blink. Copper springs popped from his torn chest panels. He raised his crooked tin hand and jerked it side-to-side.

"Um, he waved," I whispered. A metal man waved at *me*.

Mekasha retreated, arms spread wide, pushing me toward the door. Mr. Automaton moved in sync. Mekasha stopped. It stopped.

"What does he want?" I said, marveling at how awesome Mr. Automaton was.

"Not sure." Mekasha's voice remained steady. "He could be an old guard meant to scare trespassers. But I've never seen one with mechanics that are so . . . human."

We continued, and Mr. Automaton followed, waving and blinking. Mekasha flung open the door. We shoved into a half-lit hallway, kicking the door closed before Mr. Automaton could get through. A *rap-rap* hit the handle from the other side. The latch released, and the door opened. Mr. Automaton tweaked out his head and waved.

"We need to run." Mekasha yanked my hand.

I tugged him back. "Wait." An automaton of any sort was not in my story. Especially one that waved. Where had he come from? "I think he wants to help." I edged closer. "Look there. Initials *MSM* are stamped into his shoulder. Maybe it stands for *Mail Sorter Man*. He works in the mailroom."

"He *worked*," Mekasha said. "The room is abandoned."

Mr. Automaton blinked several times.

"He understands." A flutter rolled through me. He was so cool. I wanted to take him home, study his design. "Maybe he can show us the city document room."

Mekasha eyed him. "These robots don't go making pals."

I sighed. I didn't have the experience of this world like Mekasha, and maybe I should've been cautious, but somehow Mr. Automaton felt, well, almost familiar to me. "Can you take us to the document room?"

Gears spun in his chest, and he walked forward. We stepped aside to allow him by, and a *clunk clunk* came from his torso. He seized up, bending at the waist.

I tapped his back. "He won't move." Mekasha focused the flashlight on Mr. A, and a handle near the waist caught my eye. "A crank," I said.

"Yeah," Mekasha said with a snap of his fingers. "The original models were hand-cranked."

I reached for the handle, but Mekasha stopped me. "Issy, wait. These old designs aren't used anymore. Whoever cranked him up could still be around." He shone the flashlight up and down the passageway. Nobody in sight.

"Let's have Mr. Automaton lead us to the document room, fast." I grasped the handle and turned. It ratcheted several rotations. Robo-dude spasmed into an upright position, the gears in his chest whirring. I shuffled around to his front. He blinked, pointed, and continued along the hallway.

Mekasha huffed. "All right, we follow him, but ya stay close to me."

We trailed the turtle-speed of Mr. Automaton. He nodded at portraits on the walls of prior U.S. Presidents. I recognized Andrew Jackson, the seventh president, pictured on twenty-dollar bills. "Mr. Automaton is our tour guide," I laughed.

Mekasha clicked his tongue and flashed the light into

dark corners.

Mr. Automaton made one last turn before he paused at the top of a marble staircase above an impressive rotunda. His arms spread in a grand gesture at a ginormous gear rotating underneath a circular glass surface on the rotunda floor. *Whoa!* Steam spurted from the edges, triggering a team of at least a dozen clockwork hedgehogs who scurried forth with small towels to wipe the mist from the glass. They fled off to little holes in the sidewalls when done.

I giggled, despite our serious task at hand. Mom and I could totally use those hedgehogs to keep up with housework.

"This is the City Hall entrance." Mekasha's voice was sharp. "He's taking us to the security office near the front. I told ya."

Mr. Automaton shook his head and flicked his thumb to the side, then took off around the top of the stairs.

"I think he wanted to share the view from up here," I said. "He's proud of where he works."

We continued to follow Mr. Automaton until he stopped before an ornate door. He tapped the engraved script letters on its front.

I nodded like a bobblehead at Mekasha and smirked. "The documents room."

He held up his hands in defeat. "Ya be right about the old tin man."

Mr. Automaton reached into an open panel on his chest and retrieved a pin. He pushed it into the door's keyhole with a jiggle. The latch clicked, and the door swung open. He ushered us in then followed behind, securing the door closed.

Mekasha lit the bedroom-sized area with the flashlight. File cabinets lined the walls, each labeled with letters. I opened the "S" drawer. The files inside swung to a standstill. I rifled through them.

"*Nada* for Statue of Liberty." I moved over to the "L" cabinet. "No mention of 'liberty'." A tinge of fear edged into my mind. I was wrong. The blueprints weren't here.

Mekasha jogged around the room, pushing aside heavy wall curtains. "Look, a safe." He held back a curtain to reveal a bronze lockbox embedded into the wall. "I've heard the statue's design be top secret."

Yes, of course! Jocko Jones had commented on how secretive the project was. I took quick strides to join Mekasha at the oven-sized safe. A peg stuck out from a shallow indent in the center of the door where a spinning combination knob should've been.

"Hmph, the dial's missing." I waved at Mr. Automaton. "Can you open it?"

He waggled a crooked appendage at me and shook his head.

"He won't break into it. An honest clockwork," Mekasha said. "Now what?"

I pressed my fingers to my temples. In my book, Jocko didn't break into a safe to find the statue's blueprints. Instead, I had him build one to keep the designs hidden. I spent days exploring how safes were made. I hoped they all worked the same way.

"Mekasha, how many magnetic marbles do you have?"

He wrinkled his nose at me while digging a handful from his pouch. "A few. Why?"

I took two from his stash. "Electromagnetism."

"Elec-magy, what?"

"Mom and Dad talk about electromagnetism a lot. Basically,

it's magnets and electricity."

Mekasha scratched his chin. "What's electricity?"

I crinkled my brow. "Have you only jumped to times that use steam and gears?"

"No." He shrugged. "The two time periods I've been to used insects to power things."

"Insects?" Woah!

"Sure. Ya contain a few million mosquitoes. All that buzzing creates enough vibration to generate heat and momentum. But it sounds like the electricity in yer time won't give ya a bunch of itchy bumps."

I laughed. "No, it won't." Oh boy, was his science brain in for a treat the first time he jumped somewhere with electricity. "This energy is an invisible force that can power stuff, like lamps and gadgets. You don't need steam anymore." I nudged his shoulder. "It'd be great if you discovered electricity here."

Mekasha grinned his tooth-gap smile as I signaled for Mr. Automaton. "We need copper springs, please," I said.

Mr. Automaton sauntered to my side, staring at me with his eyeball-less sockets. His hand rotated into a thumb up toward his chest.

"Yes, that's good," I told him, astonished at the robot's personality.

Mekasha toyed with a pocket watch, eyeballing Mr. Automaton. "Let's find the blueprints and get outta here."

I peeked into Mr. Automaton's open panel. "Got any spare springs?"

He rummaged around his insides then produced three flexible copper coils, each about five inches long and a little larger than the diameter of a roll of quarters. He poked about his thigh and found two more. I laid the springs on a table, linking them end-to-end with a bit of copper wire from Mr. Automaton's neck, after his permission, of course.

Mekasha focused hard on what I was doing. He slapped his knee. "Like a long copper snake."

"Yes. Perfect track for a battery."

Mekasha gawked at me. "Batteries be too big to fit inside the springs."

"Yes, batteries in *this* time." I got Dad's calculator from my backpack and slipped off the cover. "Triple 'A' batteries. These are from *my* time."

I placed a magnetic marble on each end of one battery. "Electricity from the battery flows to each magnet." I inserted the first half of the battery into one end of the spring "snake." "The copper will carry the electric current from the battery and create a magnetic field because of your marbles. The magnetic field pushes the battery through the copper coils."

I released the battery. It shot through the copper springs and out the other end.

"Wow, amazing." He eyed me. "Ya sure ya ain't the same type of scientist as yer parents?"

"No, I'm an inventor and a writer. Basically, I write books that include all gadgets I hope to make someday. I want to be like Jocko, my main character. He has adventures and creates gadgets from his mind." I paused, grasping how much of Mom and Dad's science was also in my inventions. I'd learned more than I realized from their talks with me about electricity, gravity, math, centrifugal force—*mighty skyscraper!* I wasn't like Jocko;

159

I was like them.

"Hey, there." Mekasha waved his hand at my face.

"Um, yeah, I guess some of my parents' research rubbed off on me."

"Writer, inventor, scientist—ya can be all three."

His words hit me. He was so right. And I promised myself that if I got us all home, I'd show more interest in Mom and Dad's type of science. I already planned to ask them about aerodynamics after riding in the mail-toboggan contraption.

Mekasha picked up the magnetized battery. "How do we use it to open the safe?"

I signaled him to place the battery into one end of the spring track while I brought the other end around to connect. It formed a circle flush on the table. The battery traveled round and round, pushed by the magnetic field.

Mekasha's head moved with the motion. "Ya made a train."

"Yes. It's the easiest electric train to build."

I disconnected the ends, and the battery came out. "We lay the copper spring circle flat against the safe door where the dial would be. As the battery moves, the magnetic marbles pull on the dial's mechanism behind the door."

"How will we know when it hits a number in the combo?"

"The electric current should cause a crackling sound as the lock tumbler falls into place at each number." I bit the inside of my cheek. I hoped that's how it would work.

"What about turning the dial the other way for the second number?" Mekasha scratched his ear.

What had Dad said about battery ends being polar opposites? "One end of the battery is pushed by the electric current. The other end is pulled. The battery can travel in only one direction. We'll flip the copper spring track over so the battery will run the other way."

Mekasha plucked up the coils. "Let's give it a try."

We positioned the circle track against the safe's door. Mr. Automaton held it in place while Mekasha inserted the battery. I quickly connected the ends, and the battery made its way around. Squeaks and creaks came from behind the door.

"It's working." Mekasha's eyes lit up.

About three-quarters of the way, a sharp crack emitted. We took off the copper track to stop the safe's internal dial. A soft thud sounded with the first tumbler locking into place.

"Now, the other way." I flipped over the track, and Mr. Automaton held it in place. Mekasha kicked off the battery, and I closed the loop. The crackle sounded within seconds. We removed the copper track, and tumbler number two fell into position.

We turned the track one more time and repeated the steps for tumbler three until hearing the final crack. Mekasha reached for the safe handle, but then keys jingled outside the room's entrance.

My eyes bulged. "Someone's here." I looked at Mr. Automaton. "Hurry. Hold the front door closed."

Robo-dude strode over and seized the knob. A sharp pound came from the other side.

"Hey, who's in there?" a deep voice shouted.

"Faster," I pleaded with Mekasha. He cranked the safe handle, creaking the heavy lid open. His hands flew through the files inside, and he gripped a rolled parchment tinted blue.

The pounding on the room entrance deepened. "Open up!"

"Quick, Mekasha, unroll it." My heart skittered. We were so close.

He unfurled the blueprints across the table, revealing a skeleton frame of the Statue of Liberty. Something crashed outside the door, and I jumped.

"You, in there!" came the voice.

Mekasha frantically moved his fingers over the plans. "Not here, not here. The leg, the foot, here! A door behind the heel. We got it. Let's go."

We rolled the paper and shoved it back into the safe.

"Open up, or I'll blow you to smithereens!" The furious voice said.

I squeezed Mekasha's hand, my panic pinching his skin. "I don't want us to get blown up. We need to let him in."

He flinched back his arm and scanned the room. "Hide behind those."

We ran toward the door and hid behind thick drapes hanging on the nearby wall. I peeked between the seams and signaled Mr. Automaton to release the door handle. A man burst into the room, dressed in leather pants, jacket, and official insignia pins.

"A security guard," Mekasha whispered.

The guard stopped inside the threshold. His eyes flew over the room. Then he huffed at Mr. Automaton. "How dare you block a chief officer."

Mr. Automaton held up his hand to gesture defeat but then seized up.

"Worthless old bot. How'd you get cranked up anyway?" The man thunked Mr. Automaton upside the head and stomped past him further into the room. He searched the table, picking up the battery. "What do we have here?" His eyes hardened.

I cringed. I'd forgotten to grab it. Mekasha tapped my arm and threw his head toward the exit. We slinked out from the drapes and slipped out the door while the man's back was turned. I did a quick turnaround. "Thank you, Mr. Automaton," I mouthed.

He winked an eyelid.

Ah, smart. You hadn't seized up at all. I returned the wink at Mr. Automaton's clever distraction of the guard as Mekasha and I fled City Hall.

17 Blimpy Ride

I STRETCHED MY limbs awake the following morning to Professor's gentle snores from across the tent. A quick whiff of my shirt made me lower my arms. I crinkled my nose. Four days without a shower was not a sweet odor on me.

All of the chaotic events ricocheted around my head—especially last night's adventure with Mr. Automaton. Mekasha and I made a great team. I smiled at Mekasha, sound asleep on his mat near Professor. How was it possible to feel like I'd known him for years when it had only been a few days? A chill startled me as the anticipated loss settled into my soul. I shook it off. Only a couple more nights before Mom and Dad arrived on the docks. This was about rescuing them.

"*Mija*, why the frown?" Aunt Maria patted my arm. I hadn't noticed she awakened.

"Just tired, *Tía*," I squeaked.

"*Está bien,* Issy," she whispered. "The heart knows a true *amigo,* no matter the passage of time—years, months, even days." She glanced at Mekasha. "Your heart knows."

Warmth spread through me. Time didn't define friendship.

After a breakfast of eggs with *pan dulce,* Mekasha took me around the Bizarre Bazaar. We watched funny animal shows and scary sword acts. The steam-driven carousel was my favorite. I savored the day with Mekasha, stamping the memories on my mind.

We arrived at his boxcar near dusk to pick up supplies before heading back to Professor's tent. Mekasha shoved a few trinkets into his satchel for Naya, then kept busy with the star maps, jotting notes on her possible location.

"The Big and Little Dippers." He motioned me to the scope then swiped at his misty eyes. "Naya used to say she was the little one, and I was the big one, always protecting her."

I gave his shoulder a gentle tap. "You'll find her."

"Issy, ya could stay here." He nodded several times and clicked his tongue. "Help me find Naya, live with Professor and us."

Tempting for a split moment, but I couldn't bear to be without my family. I shook my head, silent.

Mekasha gasped. "What an awful thing for me to suggest. Of course, ya want to go home. I'll just miss ya a lot when ya finally get to leave. I know we'll find your parents."

I gave him a side hug, holding on a couple of extra seconds. "I'll miss you, too."

He cleared his throat and grabbed his satchel. I wiped my eyes and picked up my backpack. "Let's join Professor, Aunt Maria," I said.

Neither one of us spoke much during the trek to Professor's tent. I kept quiet, thoughtful. I didn't dare talk, or the tears would flow.

Back at Professor's, we packed a few more supplies. Galaxy and Luna settled into their jars for the night. I nestled their containers, snug inside a blanket on the floor next to my bed. The pulse of their tachyon forces comforted me like a heating pad.

With night sliding in and rain battering the tent top, we all hit the hay early. I left on my boots for our quick leave before dawn. Mekasha and I would need to wake in the ghoulish hours for the cover of darkness on our way to Bedloe's Island. My parents arrived in two nights. We couldn't fail to find Star.

A deep sleep dragged me into dreams about Mom and Dad. But then a shout woke me. In my groggy state, for a moment, I thought I was home and that it was one of Dad's super-early-morning fire drills. But I quickly startled back to reality. This wasn't home. A rough hand fisted my sleeve and yanked me to my feet.

"Get up," the voice growled above my head.

Terror stiffened my arms. My eyes strained in the dim lantern light. I slid my foot toward Aunt Maria's bed mat, and my boot tip met a solid form.

"Aunt Maria?" I nudged her with my toe, but she didn't stir. "*Tía!* Meka—"

Someone shoved a rough cloth in my mouth and wrenched my arms. I winced from the sharp pain between my shoulder blades. A scream erupted inside my voice box and sputtered through my lips.

A second person, shorter, bulkier, walked into my side vision.

I craned my head over my shoulder. Thunder boomed, and lightning flashed, illuminating the space around me. What I saw in those two seconds made me double over: Mekasha, Aunt Maria, and Professor, all lying still on the floor. The short man, wearing hoot owl goggles, hovered over them.

And the man behind me—Skull.

I jerked forward, throwing him off balance but not enough to loosen his grip on me.

"Let's go, you buffoon," Skull barked at the Hoot Owl guy.

Another lightning burst exposed the pudgy Hooty, his hand now inside the rat stew pot. He drew it out and licked his finger. "Good eats, S—"

"Shut up, you blubbery whale." Skull lunged forward and whacked him upside the head. "Grab what you found and move out. And get her backpack."

Hooty opened his mouth, letting it hang a moment but snapped it shut and dutifully picked up his knapsack and my pack. Skull whirled me around with a shove through the door.

Outside the tent, the early morning hour and new rainfall meant a deserted Merchant's Maze. Hooty tossed my bag at my feet and snarled, "I'm not carrying your load."

Skull growled at Hooty, "Lazy snucker," then picked up my backpack and shoved it onto my shoulders. He held firm to the pack and guided me past tent after tent, all closed tight, no lit lanterns, no one to help me. Near Cutter's Cut, I wished Gus would appear and ask me to come inside. I'd take him up on his offer this time.

We stopped at the edge of Bizarre Bazaar in front of an odd vehicle. A blimp-shaped canvas balloon hovered in chains above an enclosed metal box barely big enough for five or six adults. Steam poured from one end, and gears churned alongside huge cranking pistons. Rain pattered against the balloon like scurrying rats.

"Get it open," Skull ordered Hooty.

Hooty unlatched a side door, which Skull pushed me through headfirst. I knew I had to keep my cool and not provoke them to hurt me. I stumbled over the threshold and fell onto a leather bench seat against the wall, opposite the door. My backpack cushioned my landing. Suspended light bulbs flickered with the sway of the contraption, and queasiness swam my intestines.

Around me was a cozy-Grandma's-cluttered-house vibe: copper, brass, and gold surfaces, littered with switches, gears, and pulleys. Like inside the submarine from *10,000 Leagues Under the Sea*.

Skull ducked on his way in, followed by Hooty, who deposited himself on the bench across from me, next to the door. Hooty chucked his knapsack to the side and took off his spectacles. I gagged on the cloth in my mouth and yelled, but it came out a garbled mess. He snickered as he took the rag from my teeth. Now up close, I recognized him perfectly.

"Chunk!" I screamed.

"The one and only," he said, showing his rotted teeth.

"She's in with that street kid and the Professor." Skull removed his mask and tucked it underneath the bench seat.

My insides turned to mush. "Sal."

He winked, and I gritted my teeth before the shock could pop them from my mouth. Dread took over my limbs, and I struggled to remain upright. Sal was Skull and Skull wanted

tachyons. *Sal* was Boss's competition—the unknown guy Mekasha had mentioned. A double-crosser.

Sal positioned himself in a leather chair at the front control panel. He worked a series of levers, sending gears spinning and steam spurting outside in a wreath at the portholes behind Chunk's head. The blimp swayed. "Pull up the line," he called out.

Chunk lumbered over to the door and cranked a side knob. A chain rattled outside. "Good to go."

The box shuttered with the lift off the ground as if hitched to hundreds of helium balloons. A dim light shone outside the porthole from the sun inching above the horizon. We continued to rise, and the Bizarre Bazaar came into full view. I wiped my slick palms on my pants in the same frantic rhythm as my pulse. How would anyone find me?

For the rest of the journey, Chunk made a show of inhaling four grilled cheezies, licking grease off his fingers one by one. He'd shoved an extra sloppy one near my face with a triple chin-jiggle laugh. What a five-year-old. I got the urge to put him in a time-out.

After going through the elements of the periodic table six times in my head to keep myself busy, the blimp finally descended. Sal shouted to Chunk, "Hey, you whale, clean up your mess. Boss boards when we land."

Boss. I gulped so hard it hurt my throat. Mekasha had said Boss was ruthless. If I was right and Sal was two-timing this Boss as the Skull, I didn't want to be in the middle of a possible fight.

Chunk snatched up the sandwich wrappers and wiped cheese from the floor. The blimp landed with a thump. Three heavy bangs hit the door outside. I cringed. Boss sounded like a hefty guy.

"Hey there, Boss," Chunk squeaked as he opened the door.

A black high-heeled boot over a black-leather pant leg stepped inside. The person it belonged to bent to fit through the door and came in the rest of the way. No hefty man here.

Boss was a woman.

18 Boss

BOSS SNARLED HER lip at me, barely showing one tooth. Wait. Was that? A diamond-studded tooth! The hardest rock of all rocks. She could tear through meat in seconds with those chompers. Her eyes curiously examined mine as if trying to recall a memory. It made me squirm in my seat.

I caught myself gawking at her face, and I averted my stare. But her face was hard not to notice: tight, wrinkle-free, peach-pale, cat-like eyes, and a button nose (no corn cob pipe). Angled at the jawline, her straight blonde bob made the perfect frame for her wax expression. A gold decorative headpiece with gear-shaped discs on either side covered her ears, similar to wraparound ear muffs.

She waved her hand at me like I was last week's garbage. "What's this?"

Her raspy voice reminded me of my old principal, who

chain-smoked behind his car before school.

"A little insurance, Boss." Sal lingered at her side. So loyal. Yeah, right—so loyal with a skull mask hidden nearby.

She remained tight-lipped, pulling off her black leather gloves. Dark purple polish adorned her fingernails, with tiny gold chains dangling from each tip. They jangled with her hand movements. She smoothed the sleeves of her crushed velvet coat, then swung up the gloves and slapped Chunk's face.

I coiled back, clicking my number rings to calm me. She *was* ruthless.

"Ow, Boss." Chunk held his ham-sized hand over his cheek; his bottom lip thrust out. "Why'd you's do that?"

"Stupidity," she said, then glared at Sal. "Insurance means you made an error. We can't afford errors. Not with that skull guy out there taking all the tachyons."

I stiffened at Sal. He scowled at me and cracked his knuckles into a fist. A warning to keep my mouth shut. What a cheater, but I didn't dare reveal his secret in these close quarters. Things could turn ugly, and I'd lose my chance to escape.

Chunk shoved another cheezie into his mouth and shrank away from Sal's growl.

"Knock it off, imbeciles," Boss said. "You freak out over that skull bandit every time he's mentioned. Get a grip."

"Yeah, okay, Boss," Sal said in a smooth tone. "The competition makes us nervous, you know."

"Whatever," Boss huffed. "The insurance. What did you mess up?"

"Boss, take a load off." Sal patted the bench seat on the wall opposite me. "You'll like what we found."

She sat with a flick of her hand. "On with it."

Sal snapped his fingers at Chunk and pointed to the knapsack. "We got a strong hit on the tachyon sensor at the bazaar." Chunk pouted but held up the bag.

"You found more?" Boss's voice went from raspy to a high-pitch squawk.

"Not exactly." Sal motioned to Chunk. "Numbnuts dropped the detector. Broke it, but not before we traced the source to an area of three tents. Unfortunately, we didn't have time to find any vessels."

I let out a small sigh. Galaxy and Luna were safe.

Boss snarled, raising her gloves at Sal.

"Hold on." He waved his hands. "It gets better." She pursed her lips and nodded for him to continue. "We snuck into the third tent, but then Chunk tripped over some kid. The rascal got off a round with his slingshot before I gave his face a sleepy rag. He went nighty-night quick. Also gave a man and a woman rags so they wouldn't scream. We had to get out of there because of the ruckus Chunk caused."

I clenched my hands. At least Mekasha, Aunt Maria, and Professor were only in a deep sleep. Nothing worse.

"Why take her?" Boss nodded toward me.

"Like I said, insurance. We can trade her for the tachyons they must have."

She tapped her boot. "The ones you didn't find. Brilliant. What *did* you find?"

"We brought you this." Sal took out an object the size of a soccer ball from the knapsack.

I recognized the blanket around the bundle. The one from

my bed mat. What had they taken? My mind churned. No!

He pulled the blanket away to reveal two glass jars. One held Luna. The other, Galaxy. They weren't safe at all. Professor would be devastated if they got hurt.

Boss held out her hands, her face an expression of—possibly—wonder. The lack of smiley lines or frowny wrinkles made it difficult to tell.

"They are exquisite." She took the jars, placing Luna to her side before removing the lid from Galaxy's. Galaxy cowered at the bottom as Boss squeezed her fingers inside.

Luna dissolved into a clacking raucous at the sight of her cornered sister. She hung from under her jar's lid, stomping the tips of her appendages.

Boss darted her eyes to the upset butterfly. "Impressive." She tightened the lid back on Galaxy and picked up Luna's jar. "Perhaps I take out the gutsy one first."

"You leave her alone!" I lunged, and Sal held me back.

Boss took off the lid, and Luna held tight on the underside. Boss turned Luna upright, face-to-face, but pulled back as the butterfly raised her legs and aimed her antennae at Boss's nose. "Lively one, aren't you? Advanced clockwork. Look at that intricate crescent moon design." Her brow furrowed. "Who made you?"

Chunk plopped down next to Boss. "Had to be the old Professor. You's know, the one not all there in the head." He wound his finger near his ear.

A cry cut off from Boss's parted lips, and she stiffened upright in her seat. "Professor was in the tent?"

"Yeah, there with her, too." Chunk jabbed his pudgy finger toward me and snickered.

Boss whacked Chunk with a glove. "Enough." She turned to Sal. "Who are the others?"

"A street boy. And an older woman. Looks like the girl."

Boss puckered her trout lips toward me. "You jumped." Her harsh tone bit the air. Luna pranced atop the lid like she was ready to take off. "Stay put," Boss commanded with a threatening glare. Luna flicked a gear at Boss, then snapped her wings closed. Boss gave a haughty laugh and fixed her eyes on mine.

I held her gaze. Lying wouldn't work. Somehow, she knew. "Yeah, I jumped. My Aunt Maria did, too." So, there. My plan: the defiant teenager. Sometimes it worked on Mom, and she'd give up quick. No luck with Boss. She stood with Luna in hand, still sitting on the lid, and parked herself next to me on the bench. Dark speckles peppered her green eyes like a song sparrow's egg. I almost expected Boss to chirp.

"Where are the tachyons you used for your jump?" She stared me down, watching, waiting for me to slip up.

I remained silent, grateful that Chunk had broken their tachyon detector. But my moment of appreciation melted, taking my shoulders with it. Using her other hand, Boss pulled a small black box from behind the bench and set it on her lap.

"You's got a new detector." Chunk swiped his hand at it, and Boss slapped him away.

"No touchy, Chunky. It's the latest model. Can detect a much tighter area." She flipped a switch on the box, and its gears went wild. "Well, well. Quite a strong signal."

Her clover-scented perfume overwhelmed my sinuses, and my eyes watered. I sat ramrod. Mom's words swam around my head: *The mind helps the heart overcome emotion.*

Boss moved Luna closer to the detector, and the gears spun faster. "What a clever vessel."

Oh no, she figured it out. I clicked my number rings, trying to squash my panic.

Boss placed Luna back into the jar.

Chunk fell over himself while getting Galaxy's jar to Boss. He held it up. "This butterfly must be a source too." His clown-like grimace took over his face.

"Nice *guess*, Chunk-y." Boss sneered, bringing the tachyon detector toward Galaxy.

Galaxy cowered and vibrated, her wings clanking the glass like an awful alarm. "I said, leave them alone!" I reached for Galaxy's jar, only close enough for my number rings to tink against the side. The tachyon detector suddenly stopped.

Boss yanked the jar from my reach. I held out my palm to her. My fingers shook from the odd vibration coming from my rings. "Give Luna and Galaxy b-back." My voice gave me away, and I dropped my hand.

The tachyon detector's sensors kicked off again.

Boss let out a hideous laugh. She turned off the black box and clipped it to her belt, then stood with a butterfly jar in each hand. "Luna and Galaxy. Oh, Professor, so crafty to name them after your dead daughters. And to use them as tachyon vessels? Fitting." For a moment, she acted like Professor was there in front of her. Then she glared at me. "Where is *Star?*"

I gulped loud, unable to hide my shock. She knew Professor's daughters.

Her face morphed into a jack-o-lantern. "Ah, so there *is* a Star. Thank you for the confirmation." She set the jars on the seat bench across from me.

Wait. No! My insides squirmed. Boss would go after Star. She'd want all three tachyon vessels.

"We'll find the star for you's, Boss," Chunk said, slobber clinging his chin.

Boss curled her lip at him and shook her head before addressing Sal. "We go to Professor. Trade the girl for the third clockwork."

"What if he don't cooperate?" Sal lifted strands of my hair. I headbutted his hand. He promptly laughed.

"We'll let the aunt take care of it for us." Boss rubbed her palms together, rattling her nail chains.

"How's she gonna do that?" Chunk slurped in his drool.

Boss ran her finger down my cheek. "Give the aunty a choice. She gets the last butterfly from Professor, or her precious niece gets a one-way ticket to a black hole."

Blood drained from my forehead to my toes like a sheet of ice drawn over my body. Aunt Maria would never let anyone hurt me.

19 Whirly-Cycle

CHUNK PREPARED THE blimp for take-off. Boss settled in next to Luna and Galaxy's jars. She primped her face in a compact mirror then adjusted the unusual headphone device over her ears. I couldn't tell if that thing had a purpose or was a weird fashion accessory. Either way, an odd version of *Princess Leia*.

She slid off the ear apparatus and smoothed her platinum hair. Chunk asked her a question, but she didn't pay him attention.

"Come on, Boss." He waved his hands at her. "You's think the sun looks more orange today?"

She glared at him with a "Psh" before replacing the headband over her ears. Chunk plopped down to my right and huddled into his jacket like a hurt puppy.

"Back to the bazaar," Sal said. He worked several levers on the control panel. Steam spurted outside the portholes while pulleys above our heads kicked off, and the blimp lifted.

We rose high into the muted sunlight, shadowed by gloomy clouds. My mind formulated an escape plan for when we landed. A distraction would work. I could reveal Sal's identity, cause chaos between him and Boss, giving me a chance to get away. But would Boss believe me over her right-hand man? How would I grab two glass jars containing fragile clockworks and get us all out the door? Of course! One of the gadgets I'd snatched from my bedroom. Thank goodness I had my backpack.

With Sal busy at the blimp controls, Boss primping in her compact mirror, and Chunk working his way through a cheezie, I angled my back to them and slid one arm from my backpack. I pulled the bag around to my side, inching my hand into the front pocket. My fingers curled around the potassium-projectile.

The silver cylinder, the length of my palm, was a sealed CO_2 cartridge pressurized with carbon dioxide. Dad used these to pump up the tires on his bicycle. I'd attached a little metal basket, the size of a golf ball, on the end where the CO_2 comes out. Inside the basket, I tucked a baggie of potassium powder. When potassium mixes with water, it creates a mini-explosion. All I had to do was break the seal, and the CO_2 would launch the baggie. Now, I needed to wait for a water source for the potassium to connect with, and Ka-boom.

The potassium-projectile fit snug in my hand as I wiggled on my backpack and waited for our arrival to the Bizarre Bazaar. Time dragged on. I daydreamed about playing disc golf with Dad and working on hard math problems with Mom.

After singing Professor's potato song in my head a good fifty-two times, the blimp descended. Steam blasted outside the door's small window. I hoped the spray wouldn't evaporate too much by the time the exit opened.

I shifted in my seat, facing straight ahead. Sal remained preoccupied with the controls. Boss groomed herself (yes, still at it) with the butterfly jars snug at her side. Chunk pulled yet another squished cheezie from his pocket. How had he possibly fit that many? He attacked it from all angles with his rotten teeth.

The blimp thudded to the ground, and Sal snarled at Chunk, "Ready the hatch."

Boss twisted to view out the porthole behind her as Chunk lugged himself over to the door. He gripped the handle and turned until it clicked. Boss stood, leaving the jars on the bench to smooth down her hair, then tighten the laces on her boots.

My heart rocketed around my chest. This had to work. Chunk pulled the hatch open, and steam poured in. I aimed the potassium projectile into the mist and broke the seal with my nail. The CO_2 blasted the paper baggy apart, sending the potassium into the vapor. A powerful burst of pink sparks shot through the blimp in all directions, and Boss screamed.

I jumped off the bench and shoved her hard. She slammed into the metal wall, her head making an awful crunching sound before her body went limp. Chunk's face fell like a shocked bobblehead, the cheezie hanging from his mouth.

With a lunge, I swiped for the butterfly jars. Sal came at me with his dagger, but he tripped over Boss's legs, giving me a precious second. I nicked Galaxy's jar with one hand and stretched for Luna with my other. But before I could grab her jar, Sal steadied himself and slashed at me, and his knife tip ran across my arm. I recoiled sideways and flung myself through the blimp door, missing Chunk's hammy-hand. With a protective hug around Galaxy's jar, I rolled to the ground, sprang up, and ran into Merchant's Maze. I knew what it meant to have left Luna behind, and I'd have to face Professor because of it.

Over my shoulder, Sal was on my tail, but no Chunk or Boss. I wondered a moment if she were unconscious or worse. Her neck had bent at an awful angle. I skittered around shoppers, ducking in and out of tents. Sal gained on me in the straightaways. I quickly calculated the number of turns needed to lose him. Because Sal was over six feet tall, his velocity would slow with each shift of his body weight, making him fall behind.

Formulas spun in my head. I spurred myself to find Cutter's Cut, the closest tent to Professor's. Past three merchants, diagonal at Fashion Alley, sharp left at the rug stand, tight right to the food tents. I heaved myself into the rear entrance of Dougy's Dough-light Donuts and hid behind a heap of flour sacks.

My mouth gaped like a fish on dry land, sucking in air, listening. The baker hollered out prices, but I couldn't hear Sal-sized bootsteps coming my way. I inched out, peeking around the maze. With so many merchants, turns, and chaos, my only hope was that Sal couldn't remember how to find Professor's tent.

I took off between the aisles and wound my way to Cutter's Cut, making it down the stretch of tents. Within minutes, I caught sight of Professor's gray canopy. Stepping inside, out of breath, I gave Aunt Maria, Mekasha, and Professor the shock of their lives.

"*Mija!*" Aunt Maria bear-hugged me. "What happened to you?" She ran her hands over my shoulders. Her messy curls fell around her mascara-smeared eyes.

"F-fine. Need water." I glimpsed outside the tent. No Sal

yet. "We have to go."

Mekasha flung a chair around. "Sit, Issy." He scooped water from a pail with a tin cup and handed it to me. "Tell us what happened."

I cradled Galaxy's jar in the crook of my arm and gulped the not-so-fresh liquid.

Professor kneeled, taking his daughter from me. He tipped the jar and removed the lid. Galaxy crawled out to the edge and flew to his shoulder, where she nestled into his neck. His eyes pleaded with mine. "Where is Luna?"

I choked on an air bubble lodged in my throat. The thought of Professor's broken heart shook me.

"Issy, you okay?" Professor patted my shoulder. "You have Luna, right?"

"B-boss has h-her. I'm so sorry, Professor. I could only grab one jar." I buried my face in my hands to smother my sobs. I'd failed him. Would I fail Mom and Dad, too?

Professor grabbed a napkin next to him and gently wiped away the bits of blood smudged on my scratched arm. He sighed. "It's okay, child. Luna can hold her own. We'll find her."

I raised my head, and a yelp escaped from my gut. My face coiled in agony at what I still needed to tell him. I couldn't bear to cause him more pain.

"What is it?" Professor's expression mirrored my alarm.

"Boss knows about Star."

The small amount of pink left on Professor's cheeks drained away, fading his freckles. "She'll take Star."

I shook my head to stop the wave, but my words erupted like a supernova. "You're right, Professor. She knew a lot about you. About your three girls." I turned to Mekasha. "Boss knows there's another vessel, and she has a new tachyon detector. We need to get to the statue now."

Mekasha didn't ask questions. He put on his jacket, top hat, goggles, and satchel. "Let's go."

"Wait." Aunt Maria pleaded with her eyes. "I'm coming."

I clasped her wrist. "No, there's no time. You'll slow us down."

"But it's too dangerous."

"*Tía*, we don't have time to argue. Boss's goons are on their way here. They want to use me to force Professor to reveal where Star is. I can't be here. None of us should be here."

"But, but." She wrung her hands.

I hugged her quickly. "I'll be fine. You have to let me go."

Aunt Maria studied me nervously, then sighed and nodded. "*Sí*, you're right, *mija*. You can do this." She turned to Professor. "You sure Star is at the statue?"

He raised his brows. "The most logical place." Galaxy clattered from her perch. "What is it, honey?" Galaxy took flight, circling my head, then landing on my shoulder.

Mekasha clicked his tongue. "She wants to come with us."

"Galaxy, no." Professor reached for her, but the clockwork butterfly flitted over to my other shoulder and nestled into my hair.

"Okay, okay." Professor gazed at her with a grin. "You may go. Seems you've found a chance to prove yourself, littlest one."

Galaxy pranced forward, waving her wings.

"But wait." Professor rummaged around a pile of junk near his bookcase. He pulled out a thin, silvery cloth the size of a hand towel. "I wish I would have remembered this sooner. Cover

Galaxy with this. There are thousands of titanium threads woven throughout. It'll block the tachyon signal so Boss's detector can't pinpoint your exact spot."

"We'll take good care of her." I took the silky cloth. Titanium? Like my number rings? I wanted to ask questions, but time had run out. I wrapped Galaxy and slipped her into the jar, then Mekasha snuggled her into his satchel. I grabbed my mask and shoved it into my backpack.

"First, we make one stop," Mekasha said. "I got a plan for getting to the statue." He turned to Professor and Aunt Maria. "Head to Cutter's Cut. Gus will hide you. He owes me."

Professor nodded. "We'll grab a few items here, then leave. Now get."

I followed Mekasha from the tent, my tummy fluttering with relief. He'd get us to Bedloe's Island.

THE SUN HOVERED high over the boxcar. Mekasha led me to a wooded area behind his home, where he quickly pulled large leafy branches off a huge contraption he'd been hiding. I'd never seen anything like it, a sort of bicycle-helicopter vehicle, complete with blades up top and landing skids below.

He swept out his arm. "Behold, my whirly-cycle." Patting the leather chairs in the two-seater compartment, he said, "Comfy and stylish. Come, sit."

"Wow, it's cool." I skirted to the opposite side then climbed between the crisscrossed bars, plopping into a seat. Bars also made up the floor, giving a good view of the chains running from a wheel at the contraption's front, underneath us, to the rear. I pushed out my feet to the pedals.

"Yeah, that be it." Mekasha pointed. "Put yer feet there. We'll power the whirly together."

I plunked my boots onto the pedals and peered out the front. It had fewer bars, but still, with this much metal, I had doubts we'd get the machine off the ground. I positioned my goggles over my eyes.

Mekasha crawled into his seat. He pushed on a handle sticking up from the floor between his legs. "Okay, I'm ready."

I searched for my handle. "Where's mine?"

"Ya don't have one." He winked. "I do the steering."

"You have a driver's license?" I teased. He tilted his head side-to-side, weighing his response. "Ah, never mind. Steer away." He pedaled a few rotations, and I followed his example. Above us, a twin blade jerked into action with an achy creak.

"Keep going." He thrust his legs.

My fingers grasped the cage frame, and I pushed my feet. The blade gained speed. Our legs cycled in sync, and the cage jumped a foot off the ground. We landed, giving my teeth a rattle.

Mekasha twirled his hand. "Faster."

Perspiration slickened my forehead, and my legs burned from how hard I pushed. If I had gone any faster, I would've given myself a sweat shower. Another push of my feet, and the whirly lifted again. Mekasha heaved the handle to the left, elevating us higher. My legs pumped harder.

"We caught a good draft," Mekasha said. "Keep going."

The whirly's blades spun like a pinwheel. We soon soared

over the boxcar, and a breeze propelled us ahead.

"Ya did it, Issy. We're flying in the jet stream. Ya can rest into an easy pedal."

"With pleasure." I couldn't contain my smile, no care if a handful of bugs splattered my teeth. "It's a cool flying thing."

He gave me a sideways glance. "It's a *whirly-cycle*."

"Who built it?"

"I did. By myself. Two people need to operate it, so this is her maiden voyage."

I choked on my spit. "You've never flown it before?"

"Nope. Yer the first co-pilot." He tipped his hat.

"I'm honored." And a little terrified, but I settled into a rhythmic pedal. It was a thrill, us together, the first to fly his invention. He trusted me to help operate his masterpiece.

In about a half-hour, we were above New York City. People bustled in the steam-clouded streets, unfazed by a flying go-cart-cycle. Mekasha steered us toward the murky waters of the Upper New York Bay.

A cold air blast stung my face. I shrank into my jacket to control my chattering teeth. "Um, M-Mekasha, what if we can't keep the whirly out of the water?"

He licked his finger and held it up. "The jet stream is heading straight to Bedloe's Island. We should make it, but if we start to fall, then pedal faster."

Uh, sure, no problem. My insides tightened like a little kid squeezed inside a cabinet for a game of hide-and-seek.

We approached the docks and skimmed over five steam-powered boats. Seals barked at us from atop boulders; the stench of rotten fish around their flippers hit me full-on. I gagged, then

the whirly dipped dangerously low.

"Pedal harder, Issy."

I exhaled and pushed my feet. The pulley belts squeaked in pain, but the whirly boosted several feet higher.

The island came into view. The statue's torch burned in the morning sun.

"Where will we land?" I said. Our plan to arrive in the dark hadn't worked out.

Mekasha shielded his eyes toward the statue. "Close to the heel. Boats in the harbor shouldn't see the whirly-cycle from there."

We approached the statue. I marveled at her shiny, copper penny surface. The years had oxidized the metal to sea green by my time. Even the miniature statues in the gift shops of New York wore a turquoise sheen.

Mekasha steered us to the statue's front base. I squeezed my head through the whirly's frame for a view. The figure stood on an enormous brick pedestal atop an eleven-sided star-shaped structure. Broken chains lay near her huge sandaled foot. I recalled a tidbit of information from history class: the statue's designer meant for the busted chains to represent freedom from slavery.

"The building used to be U.S. Army Fort Wood," Mekasha called out. "Then the island was picked for the *Statue of Liberty Enlightening the World*. That's her official name." He aimed the whirly around the statue's side. "Okay, slow, slow."

I eased up on the pedals, and he veered toward Liberty's rear foot. The raised heel made a nice niche to conceal us. Mekasha lowered the vehicle, landing near a fold in the statue's dress robes.

"Ya see the metal door there?" He crawled out from his

seat and ran to the heel, opening the statue's hidden entrance. Mekasha stuck his head in and out. "All clear. There shouldn't be any builders since it's the weekend. Follow me."

We stepped across the threshold. A chill settled into my bones from the icy air trapped inside the metal walls. I pulled out my mask and slipped it on to help warm my face. Faint clicks sounded from Mekasha's bag. He patted the outside. "It's okay, Galaxy. We'll find Star soon."

The ceiling slanted down as we walked along the wall. I guessed we were near where the top of the foot sloped to meet the toes. We hung a left to find the statue's center, and Mekasha pointed out a hanging sign with a short phrase. One hundred fifty steps to the head?

The words trampled over me, and I slapped my hand to my chest. "Are you kidding? That's like ten stories." My legs were still jelly from pedaling to get here.

"Hope ya got yer walking shoes on."

"No. No, I don't." I could barely make it up the stairs to my bedroom.

Mekasha retrieved Galaxy from her jar and removed the titanium cloth. "We're miles away from Boss and her detector. She can't detect Galaxy's tachyons this far." Galaxy settled onto his shoulder as we set off up the stairs. A slight dread draped me, and I silently prayed we'd find Star. She was my only chance of getting home. What if someone else had already found her?

20 Metal Beast

WE STARTED UP the tight spiral staircase, slow for the first twenty steps. I paused to gulp air and adjust my mask. Mekasha tapped his boot, his words coming out with each bounce of his foot. "Let's go, Issy. We need to get back to Professor and yer aunt. Make sure they're safe."

Galaxy waved her wings at me in encouragement. Sweet little girl. The sight of her and Mekasha waiting, depending on me. It gave me an imaginary kick in the bum. I hitched up my backpack and pushed through the burn in my thighs. At step ninety-nine, a muffled shout rose from below.

"A man." Mekasha held still.

Another shout. This time a woman.

"Boss found us." I crouched on the step. "How'd her tachyon detector reach this far?"

"I don't know. There's no detector that powerful. Come on.

It'll take them a while to get up here." He took off at a jog, me half-running after him. Saliva pooled in my mouth in a weak attempt to quench my thirst. At the 140-step mark, I tripped on a step's edge and stopped to rest. Mekasha pointed to a cutout in the platform above our heads where the stairs led. "We're almost there." He climbed the last steps through the hole and disappeared from view.

I grasped the rail, huffing and puffing my way up the final climb, then emerged onto a catwalk of wide metal planks circling the inside perimeter of the statue's head, level with the top of the mouth. My boots clumped over bits of rope and rods cluttering the walkway. I joined Mekasha in front of the statue's face. It was like looking into a cake mold.

He spread his arms between the eyes, panting. "A good three feet from eyeball-to-eyeball." Galaxy stretched her wings, helping him measure.

I could barely speak at first; I was so exhausted. I blew out a deep breath and finally was able to get out, "Check the nose for Star." I glanced back at the floor hole, certain Boss's button nose would poke through.

Mekasha bent over a railing and patted the inside of a hollow nostril. "Nothing here."

"Hey!" came the man's shout again.

I peeked over the platform. Chunk's puffy, drenched face came into view. He leaned out halfway up the spiral staircase. "I told you's they were up there."

"Outta my way." Sal shoved Chunk aside on his sprint. With his long legs and muscles, it wouldn't be long before he reached us.

"Hurry, Mekasha." I pressed up against the wall.

He leaned halfway inside the other nostril. "Nothing." He climbed inside for a better look.

My head ached. I turned toward the wall and bowed my forehead to the cool copper surface. The pain in my skull sharpened. I kicked a dusty bucket in hopes of releasing stress. The bucket clattered along the wall underneath a nostril, striking a metal panel. A white string popped from its seam. It stood out among the grimy remnants left by the workers. White string? *Can make you sing.* Professor's song!

I crouched and yanked on the cordage. A trap door in the wall slid open. Inside sat a metal puzzle box, double the size of a Rubik's Cube. *It's made from titanium.* My skin tightened with a rush of adrenaline. Star had to be in there. I snatched the vessel, but an awful thought trickled my mind. Would Professor still let me take Galaxy to get my family home now that Boss had Luna? He'd lost one daughter and may not be willing to let Galaxy go. I'd need Star. Mekasha wouldn't have any tachyons to save Naya.

Should I save four people or one?

A swell of tears burned behind my eyes, and I swallowed hard. There was no other choice. I stuffed the puzzle box in my jacket and placed my arm to hide the bulge, then nudged the trap door closed with my boot.

Mekasha wobbled out from the nose.

"Find anything?" My vocal cords quivered.

"Nah." He wiped his hands on his pants. "Ya see anything around the walls?"

His unquestioning expression weakened my legs. Mom's

voice floated in my memory, *Hacer lo correcto, pase lo que pase: do the right thing no matter what.* My shattered heart stabbed me from the inside. If keeping Star meant saving my family, then why did I feel like an awful friend?

"No, n-nope, *nada.*" I pushed my mask tight to my face, trying to hide my shame. Blood rushed my ears, drowning Mom's voice. The word "horrible" looped my mind.

"Everything okay?" Mekasha eyed me.

I couldn't tell him about the puzzle box. I needed it. I wanted my family more than anything. "Yeah, um—" I stopped, startled by a head appearing through the scaffold hole.

"Found you." Sal gritted his teeth and shimmied his shoulders through the hole, his chest heaving up and down. He stomped his way up the last rung until he stood on the platform only ten feet away.

Mekasha slid in front of me as a shield while Boss finished climbing the ladder, followed by—no!

I let out a cry.

"Aunt Maria, Professor!" I took two steps, but Boss swaggered to the center and blocked me.

Professor bent over, huffing and struggling to take in air.

"*Estoy bien, mija,*" Aunt Maria grunted out. Her wrist bangles clattered from her hand frantically waving across her face and the other clutching her purse strap that crossed her chest.

My heart went wild at the object on Boss's shoulder. "Luna!"

Poor Luna clattered into a fuss, held back by a tiny chain anchored from her wing to a rivet on Boss's jacket.

Boss wiped at the sweat on her forehead and inhaled deeply. She traced my line of sight. "Ah, yes, I've got the feisty sister." She laughed a horrible scratchy cackle then threw her chin at my *tía* and Professor. "Finding them was a breeze. Gus at Cutter's Cut loves money." Her words oozed with sarcasm. "After Professor saw his precious *Luna,* it didn't take much to make him sing. He spilled your location like a tipped garbage pail."

Galaxy clanked up a raucous from Mekasha's shoulder while Professor stood silent, robot-like. He was so subdued they hadn't bothered tying his hands or Aunt Maria's.

Mekasha balled his fists. His eyes darted from Professor to Boss. "What did ya do to him?"

Boss snickered. "Oh, a little 'ole threat to kill you all."

That set Luna off again. She clicked and clacked in the wing-cuff. Galaxy zoomed off Mekasha's shoulder, aiming at Boss's face. She wing-sliced Boss's forehead on a pass-by.

"No, Galaxy!" I yelled. She wanted to help, but it was too dangerous.

Boss gasped. She swiped her face and stared at the red stain on her fingers. "You little twit." She glared at Galaxy, eyes stern on the butterfly zooming in for another strike. Boss swung her hand, slamming the back of it into the youngest sister. Galaxy soared several feet and smacked the wall above my head. She landed with an awful crunch on the floor.

Professor snapped from his stupor. "What have you done?" He pushed past Boss and rushed to his daughter. She twitched on the catwalk, inches from the edge. He scooped her up and cuddled her to his chest. "This isn't the way!" He screamed at Boss like she had a clue to what he meant. Poor Professor. It was too much for him. For anyone.

A flicker of sadness tweaked Boss's face, but she recovered

and straightened the contraption over her ears. "I know what needs to be done."

Aunt Maria shoved Chunk aside to get to Professor. She spun around on Boss, her face twisted in hatred. "You monster!"

"Tsk, tsk." Boss waved her hand. "A worthless machine." She glanced at Galaxy, and her face faltered. She must've realized she might have ruined a tachyon source.

Galaxy. Timid, selfless Galaxy. She'd stepped up to save her sister, and now she lay in a heap in Professor's hands. He tucked his daughter inside his coat pocket, his sobs bouncing off the copper walls. There was no way I could take Galaxy on a jump.

Boss pointed at me with one of her long-nailed fingers, chain dangling. "Where's Star?"

I pulled my jacket around my waist and glanced at Mekasha, but he kept his hardened eyes on Boss. I deadened my voice. "We didn't find her."

"She lies." Sal held up the new tachyon detector from the blimp. "Strong force here." He threw a heartless look at Luna, still a prisoner on Boss's shoulder. "More than the two we already have."

Mekasha tilted his head at me. He studied my clothes, the way I held my arms around my middle. I couldn't meet his gaze. My cheeks burned, roasting me for betraying him.

I focused on Boss, grateful to hide behind my mask. It made the lie easier. "I, we didn't find anything."

"Enough stalling." Boss's icy tone cut the air.

It was a standoff: Boss, Sal, and Chunk hovered at one end of the catwalk. Mekasha, Professor, Aunt Maria, and I stood at the other end, near the statue's face. They were only two Sal-body-lengths away.

Sal held out the tachyon detector toward me. It buzzed and whined in fury.

I raised my hand in a weak attempt to block him from moving toward us. There had to be a way to get out of this. I clicked my number rings over and over, thinking, planning, formulating.

"Hey, piece of junk." Sal slapped the side of the detector. "It stopped working."

"Never mind that." Boss snapped her fingers. "We know little missy here has Star. If you don't hand over the butterfly tech, then I'll make you." She pursed her lips and let out a shrill whistle.

A horrible clattering came from below the stairs.

"Oh, you's in for it now," Chunk whooped, his fist pointed at me. He and Sal backed away from the hole in the catwalk.

I watched the opening, wide-eyed, then stiffened. Steam poured out, bringing with it a battered, rusted head. The thing scrabbled up, eyes set on me. I backed up to the wall.

A mechanical dog.

Mekasha's hand flew to his slingshot, and Aunt Maria nestled me to her side. "What is that?" she half choked.

"Say hello to Fred." Boss casually introduced her pet. "He's, shall I say, almost friendly."

The beast growled and pawed at the ground, rattling the metal sheets over its body. His nailed claws scraped notches into the platform.

Fred's eyes devoured me as Boss patted his head and whispered in his ear. She held out her palm to me. I froze. She wanted me to hand over Star. Her mouth moved, but I couldn't make out the words. Blood rushed my ears. She pushed her hand even further, but I didn't budge.

Another harsh whistle. Steam spurted from Fred's nostrils above bared razor teeth. The dog lunged. I dropped to my bottom and huddled into a ball. Mekasha shot marble after marble, but the glass spheres tinked off Fred's armor.

Then, a blaze of red and brown at my side. A wild scream.

"Not my *mija!*" Aunt Maria leaped like a *Lucha Libre* wrestler. She tackled the mechanical dog into a chokehold. A harsh bang vibrated the scaffold, and we all grasped the rails.

The dog wretched its head around and clamped its teeth on her arm. The bone-breaking crunch, mixed with her death-shriek, almost made me pass out.

"No!" I made a move, but Mekasha blocked me and lunged for Aunt Maria. I swayed with dizziness. My eyes blurred, making the air around my *tía* shimmery.

Mekasha grabbed for Aunt Maria's skirt, but it slipped from his fingertips. He slammed onto the catwalk, half over the edge, throwing his arm around a post to stop his fall into oblivion.

Aunt Maria's cries rose around us. My ears rang from the chaos.

Professor picked up a metal pipe and shouted at Boss, "Call off your dog! Don't be like this!" He brought the pipe down on the dog's back, but it bounced off with a sharp clang, and he staggered back.

The machine dog let go of Aunt Maria's bloody wrist and turned its head, snorting, growling, aimed at me. My *tía* let out a primal scream and wrapped her arms around the automaton dog again in a bear hug. Her eyes locked on mine, bottom lip quivering. She gave one nod. "Be strong, *mija*."

Then she barrel-rolled over the side, taking the metal monster with her.

21 FORGIVENESS

AUNT MARIA'S MASS of fluffy dark hair was the last thing I saw. Her screams faded as mine grew louder. I dropped to my knees.

"No! *Tia!*" I rocked side-to-side, heaving with uncontrollable sobs. Aunt Maria was dead because of me. Misery seared my chest. Dad would be devastated. His only sister. How could I have let this happen?

Mekasha sidled up to me. His arm shot around my shoulders. "Issy, Issy," he whispered in my ear. "We must leave."

I lifted my head to a loud commotion.

Professor advanced and screamed at Boss, "You took my Maria!"

She backed up until she hit the wall, hissing at Sal to help, but he stood to the side with a bored grin. No doubt, he hoped Professor would take care of his dirty work and get rid of Boss before she found out he was Skull.

Up against the wall, Boss huddled into herself as Professor yelled at her over and over, his pipe raised. Then he dropped the pipe to turn his attention to Luna and quickly unhooked her from the wing-cuff. Boss snapped out another command for Sal to attack.

Sal responded with a deeper smirk and didn't move. He watched Professor face Boss again, shouting at her. She sidestepped, trying to escape, but Professor followed her moves. She glared at Sal then called out, "Chunk-y, come help me."

Chunk dragged his eyes between Sal and Boss. Sal growled, sending the pudgy lackey recoiling in humiliation.

"Chunk-y," she said sweetly, bugging out her eyes at him. "Come help me, son."

Her portly minion's face broke into a giddy schoolboy smile.

Sal rolled his eyes and grabbed Chunk's shoulder to hold him back. "Fine, fine, I got you, Boss." He stepped closer and punched Professor in the gut.

Professor plunged to his rear, snuffles taking over his face. "Evil woman," he howled. Professor crab-walked backward, spitting out foul names to Boss until he reached us.

"Enough!" Boss caught her breath and smoothed her hand down her neck. She turned on her goons. "Took you long enough."

Chunk sulked, about to speak, but Boss waved him off as she adjusted gears on each side of her headphones. Wait, I hadn't noticed the dials before. Was it more than a fashion accessory? Could it be—?

I leaned in, whispered to Mekasha, then whispered down to Professor before taking a few steps toward Boss.

"Hey," I forced my voice, trying to hold in the hysteria over Aunt Maria's death.

"What do we have here?" Boss squared off, but Sal moved in. "No." She held out her arm. "The sassy little busybody is mine."

That was it! I raised my hand to my face. My fingers inched around the edge of my mask, and I pulled it off, down to my side. Ready. Boss already took my *tía*. She would not hurt my friends. *Bring. It. On.*

Chunk offered an onslaught of snide comments. His words bounced off me: "Ooo, scary. You's a big girl now?" My eyes locked onto Boss, and I willed my mind to overcome the fear in my heart.

"That's rich." Boss sneered at me, looking at the mask in my hand. "You pick now to get all tough. Good. It's more fun to see the face I'm about to destroy."

Mekasha gave my shoulder a gentle squeeze. Mekasha—the one I could count on. The one who I'd kept Star from.

With a quick clank of my number rings to calm my broken heart, I steadied my voice. "No, you won't destroy me. I've overcome."

"What could a girl like you possibly overcome?" Boss folded her arms and tapped her nails on the metal rivets of her jacket sleeves, waiting for my response.

I gripped my mask and raised my chin. No longer would I hide behind a story, a mask, or even a lab. The real reason I avoided making friends—so I didn't have to risk being rejected. I glanced at Mekasha. He was my people.

I squared off to Boss and yelled, "Everyone!"

As Boss smirked at my declaration, I quickly estimated the distance between us and calculated my throw power. I flexed my arm, pulled back, and flung out my hand. My mask flew, arcing at the perfect angle in the most important disc golf throw I'd ever made. It spun through the air, bashing Boss upside her head and knocking off her headphones.

Mekasha shot off two marbles and struck Sal and Chunk in the temples. They dropped like sacks of potatoes. Mekasha ripped off his top hat and jammed it over Boss's head, pulling it down so far it concealed her face. A quick tug on the buckled strap around the brim made it impossible for her to remove it. He moved on to tie up her two men.

"Sal! Chunk!" Boss staggered, yanking on the hat suction-cupped to her plasticky face.

"How do you like it now?" Professor blasted at her. Boss slammed her boots on the catwalk. Professor bared his teeth and screamed into the hat around her face. "I said, how do you like it now? Answer me!" His voice vibrated throughout the statue's head.

Boss didn't flinch, didn't pause. She continued to pull on the hat, her screeches muffled by the fabric.

"She can't hear you, Professor." I tugged on his sleeve. "That contraption she wore around her ears is a hearing device."

His brows raised while he processed the information, and his jaw slowly slackened. His face softened for some reason. "What has she done? Why? Why?" Professor patted Boss's head like a child and retreated near the wall.

The sudden change in his manner made my thoughts swirl. Who cared if she had a hearing problem—didn't Boss deserve punishment for what she did to my family and little Galaxy? I questioned Mekasha with a sigh.

He paused his tying up of the unconscious goons, and his eyes flashed at me with sympathy.

I walked over to Boss. She pressed her palms against the statue wall like she was preparing to escape. My heartbeat slowed, aching over Aunt Maria. I got close to Boss's face and whispered, "I'll never be like you."

Boss cocked her head like a bird. "Is that you, *Issy?*" She spat my name through the hat with fake laughter. "You figured out my secret. But I can still sense you, little girl." Her hand reached for me. I leaned away. Her nails grazed my chin. "What revenge have you planned for me, Issy?"

Mekasha jumped to his feet and squeezed between Boss and me. "Leave her." He clasped my hands in his while Boss slid down the wall to the floor. "Ya take Luna for the time jump if it's okay with Professor."

My breath hitched. "You'd give me the only tachyon source? What about your sister?" I was terrible for hiding Star from him. I didn't deserve even a fifth of a tachyon.

"Yes, Issy. I'd give it up for ya, my friend. I'll find Naya another way."

I swallowed against the lump in my throat, extinguishing whatever little words would never be enough to express how grateful I was. Instead, I squeezed Mekasha's hands, and he grinned.

"What about Star?" Professor's focus came off Boss, quick like a child's interest in one toy to the next. He scurried around to the statue's nose and yelled inside each nostril. "Star! Where are you?"

Mekasha joined him. "I'll help you, Professor. We'll find her." He prepared to climb up to one of the statue's eyes.

Guilt punched me in the gut. "Wait!" A dread chilled me to the bone. I was about to lose them. They wouldn't forgive me for this. Professor and Mekasha turned, and their bewildered, innocent expressions broke me. I exploded, sobbing like a blubbery Chunk. "I found her. I'm sorry. I'm so sorry."

Mekasha ran to my side. "Found who? Star?"

I held my face in my hands. "Yes. Star. I found her."

He gasped and backed away.

Professor came to me and patted my arm. I raised my eyes to him. His gentle touch reminded me of Dad. "Where is my daughter, Issy?" Luna, perched on Professor's arm, flagged her wings at me with urgency.

I slid the puzzle from my jacket and handed it over. Mekasha huddled next to Professor, giving me a narrowed glare.

Professor's face twitched into a slight smile. He made quick work of the box, depressing rivet buttons and flicking levers. Gears creaked, chains rattled. He held it out in his palm. We stared in awe as the lid sprung open, and we waited for another wonderful sister to come out of confinement.

TING!

A clockwork butterfly flew up in a twirl with a burst of sparks, spread her wings, and sailed down, landing on Professor's hand—Star. "Welcome home, my love," he whispered.

Star waved her silver-sparkled wings, etched with tiny stars and swirls. Luna sidled over to her. They touched wings in a butterfly hug.

"It's been a long while, daughter." Professor held up his hand, and Star fluttered her antennae. "Hello to you, too," he chuckled. "What's that? Galaxy?" Professor's cheeks dropped. "Oh, honey, your littlest sister isn't w-well."

Mekasha placed his hand on Professor's shoulder. "But we'll fix her." His eyes flashed annoyance at me. "I won't disappoint ya, Professor."

I wanted to explain about Star, but Boss's shout broke the moment.

"What are you going to do with me?" For the first time, her voice hitched. Her plastic façade was cracking.

Mekasha wouldn't look at me as he took out some rope. "We leave her."

"Come on now." Boss laughed with hesitation through the top hat's fabric. "What are your plans for me? Can't finish the job, can you, *Issy?*" Mekasha pulled her hands together and quickly knotted the rope around her wrists. He took the hat off her head and returned it to his own. Boss blinked, focusing on me. I turned away, heading to the stairs, and she called out, "Fine, leave me here, little girl. I hope you don't miss your auntie too much."

I flung around, charging at her. "How dare you!"

Mekasha caught me. "No, Issy, we must leave." His grip pressed into my bicep.

I took ragged breaths, my teeth clenched. It took a few moments, but I finally released my jaw. "Fine." My shoulders loosened, and my eye caught Boss's ear device a few feet away. She saw it, too. I bent down to grab it, and her face screwed up at me.

"Go ahead. Throw it over the edge," she said, her voice hitching. "It will make you feel better."

Boss's eyes grew wide as I shuffled to the edge. I held the device over the railing, but then Aunt Maria's smiling face flashed in my mind. I closed my eyes and imagined her speaking one of her favorite words: *perdón*. She had the most forgiving heart of anyone I knew.

I sighed, opened my eyes, then pivoted and squatted in front of Boss. Her eyes narrowed to slits, and she flinched when I slipped the hearing device around the back of her head and over her ears.

She sputtered, "Why?"

I stood and gazed down at her. "Because I forgive you." Aunt Maria would have done the same.

I spun on my heel and descended the spiral staircase behind Professor and Mekasha in the lead. With each step, I wouldn't dare look over the railing. No one did. I couldn't bear the thought of seeing Aunt Maria's body.

22 Assassin Bugs

PROFESSOR'S WEEPING GREW louder with each step down the stairs. He mumbled Aunt Maria's name over and over. I gripped the railing, counting down from one-hundred-fifty. A sliver of terror snaked around my belly at the twentieth step. I couldn't bring myself to peer below at what would be an unbearable scene. I didn't want to remember Aunt Maria that way.

"Hold on," Mekasha said from the step below Professor. Concern etched lines between his eyes. "Ya, both wait here. I'll go and cover Maria. Ya shouldn't see her."

I choked on the sadness and my heart-wrenched guilt. Even after keeping Star from Mekasha, he still wanted to protect me.

"No, boy," Professor said. "Too heavy a burden. Let me do it."

Luna and Star fluttered to my shoulders. They tickled my neck with their antennae, radiating their gentle energy.

Mekasha's chest expanded. "We do it together, Professor." He stretched out and clasped my hand. I instantly understood—he'd forgiven my betrayal. *Perdón.* "I'll let ya know when to join us," he said to me.

I sat on a step. My chin trembled so badly I had to grab it, holding it in place before my teeth chattered out of my mouth. Tightness took over my chest. I sucked in air, picturing Aunt Maria's smile. The *tap-tap* of Mekasha's boots echoed below me, calming my anguish. I counted each step, the math in my head computing the speed they'd arrive at the body. My naval squirmed. Five, four, three, two—

"Issy!" Mekasha's voice cracked. "Come quick!"

I jumped up, and my feet carried me two steps at a time, startling Luna and Star into flight. Was Mekasha okay? Professor? "I'm coming. I'm coming!"

I hopped the last three steps, almost plowing into Professor, who picked at a mess of metal on the floor. The mechanical dog lay sprawled on its side, his head a few feet away from its mangled legs. Confusion flooded my mind.

"Where's Aunt Maria?" I ran around the base of the statue in a blur. "Where's her body?"

Professor caught me on my second lap. "She's not here, child."

"Impossible." I bent over to collect my thoughts. "Wait, one of Aunt Maria's bracelets." I snatched up the bangle and slipped it onto my wrist, then made the sign of the cross. "She was here. But there's no way she walked from that fall." My head swam, and I began to hyperventilate. Someone must have dragged her body away!

Mekasha took my hand. "It's okay. Breathe, Issy. We've no idea what happened to her."

Anger spilled from my core, oozing up my chest to the tips of my ears. "I'll tell you what happened. Boss took her."

"She couldn't have." Professor pointed above. "She's tied up." Sobs wracked my chest. He wrapped his arm around my shoulder. "There, there, Issy."

Mekasha handed me a handkerchief, and I wiped my nose. "How could—" Pain from a mondo headache streaked behind my eyes. I pressed my hand to my forehead.

"Issy, ya okay?" Mekasha offered his hand to help steady me.

"Yeah. Another headache." I closed my eyes to the same throbbing as when I'd arrived in 1886.

A screech sounded overhead, followed by pounding footfalls. My eyes grew wide at Mekasha and Professor while Luna and Star hid behind Professor's jacket collar.

"They got out of their ropes." Mekasha tugged my arm. "We gotta leave now, Issy. Lay low in the boxcar, focus on the plan for yer family tomorrow."

A double whammy of agony plowed my heart. Aunt Maria was gone, and soon, I'd have to leave my friends.

Shouts above spurred us on. We exited the statue to find Boss's blimp hovering a few feet from the base's edge. What I wouldn't give for a set of lawn darts to take out that thing, but we didn't have time to disable her ride. I beelined to the whirlycycle with Mekasha. His frantic hands checked over the blades, chains, and levers.

"Did they damage it?" Professor jogged up with his girls tucked into his jacket. Their antennae wiggled out from his pockets.

"No, it's all in working order," Mekasha said. "They didn't bother to sabotage it."

"Boss wouldn't have thought we could escape from her," I said, grateful for one small victory. But my celebration ended at Boss's yelling. Her shouted commands from inside the statue cut through the metal sheeting. "We need to move." I waved my hand at the whirly. "Where will Professor sit?"

"In the co-pilot's seat," Mekasha said.

"And I ride where?"

"The net." Mekasha threw himself to the ground, worming underneath the whirly-cycle. He opened a small side compartment, pulled out a large mesh square, and clamped its four corners to eye-holes in the landing skids.

My heart thudded. "That doesn't look safe."

"Issy, we don't have time." Mekasha wiggled out. He guided Professor to the passenger side. "Hop in." He ran to me. "We'll raise the whirly, then ya climb into the net."

"But, I." The saliva fled from my mouth, drained out like a tart lemon sucking me dry.

"No time." Mekasha squeezed into his seat and gave Professor the signal to pedal. The whirly-cycle rose a few feet, allowing the net to open underneath like a hammock.

"Stop her!" Boss burst through the door behind the statue's heel, her minions close behind.

They caught up. Chunk flung himself at me, tripping on a workman's stray hammer. He flopped to his belly, and Sal vaulted off his rear with a hard bootstep but wobbled to the side and fell.

I shimmied into the hammock with a silent prayer for the

net to hold. The whirly-cycle dipped with my weight. Mekasha and Professor struggled to lift us off the ground.

Sal readied himself to pounce again.

I frantically pointed at him and yelled to Boss, "Skull—"

But Skull roared over my voice, "I got her!" He stumbled, looking back at Boss for her reaction to my reveal. She waved him on with an impressive grin, and he snarled at me, "Nice try."

It didn't matter. I'd startled Sal, messing him up long enough to give us the few seconds we needed. Mekasha and Professor pedaled hard, raising us into the other side of the jet stream that would shoot us back toward the docks.

I waved wildly at Sal, throwing him a smile the size of the solar system. My hair whipped around my face. I pulled down my goggles over my eyes and watched Boss's situation. Sal guided her and Chunk onto the blimp. Mist whooshed up from her steam-powered airship, and it didn't take long before they maneuvered into pursuit.

"Faster!" I yelled. The blimp gained on us, less than ten whirly-cycle lengths behind. I peered up at Professor. His reddened cheeks bloated with the strain of pedaling. How would he keep up?

I gripped the net and waited. Waited for the nightmare to end. Expecting to find it was a dream, and Aunt Maria was alive, safe, at home. We took a nosedive, and the dreamy thoughts fled my mind. My tummy roiled with the motion.

"Hang on!" Mekasha tweaked the lever. "They're shooting Assassin Bugs at us."

"Assassin what?" My already queasy insides loosened at the thought of a bug slaying me, and I threw up all over the net. I

tried to pull it together, but my head swam. A hissing hotness passed my head, and I shrieked.

"Don't let the beak of those bugs hit ya. They carry poison." Mekasha swerved to the left. The whirly-cycle caught into a doozy of a stream, jetting us at roller-coaster speeds. I laid back in the net (yeah, on the upchuck pieces) and screamed. Not a ha-ha-this-roller-coaster-is-great scream but an all-out I-was-about-to-fall-from-a-helicopter scream.

We slowed to a swift glide, and Mekasha eased up on the pedals to give Professor a rest. Sweat glistened their faces like rain on a windshield, and Professor's head lolled to the side. Behind us, the blimp hadn't made it into our current. It bobbed like a rubber ducky in disturbed waters.

Mekasha threw his fist into the air. "The blimp is caught in downward pressure. They can't catch up."

We glided further away from Boss and back to New York City, no soldiers in sight. I relaxed into my airborne sling with a deep inhale of sea mist. The moon shone like a pale disc in the dusky sky—almost-full waxing gibbous. My parents would arrive tomorrow night.

One chance to save Mom and Dad. The only chance to keep the wormhole open so we could go home. Professor's girls were worn, though. Would he give them up? Or would we be stuck in 1886?

23 Wormhole Ready

WE SETTLED INTO Mekasha's boxcar, not much appetite for dinner. The ginormous gap left by Aunt Maria sucked us all into a silent stupor. Professor slumped in the armchair, eyes lowered, tinkering on Galaxy while her sisters lingered on the armrests.

I pushed myself from the couch and joined Mekasha at his telescope. "See anything neat out there?"

He turned away from the eyepiece. "Nothing new. The same as last month, this time." He shaded in a few stars on the transparent parchment paper laid out on his desk. The diagram displayed familiar constellations, the Big and Little Dippers, the North Star, with today's date.

"What are you looking for?" I tapped my toe against the desk leg in rhythm with the tings of shame strumming through me. I'd watched him with the scope many times but never bothered to ask what he searched for. My thoughts always focused on finding tachyons.

His eyes darkened. "Naya."

"In the stars?" What did that have to do with his sister?

"Yeah, sorta. I watch for unexpected changes in the star patterns. They were created in predictable formations and repeated movements."

"Why would they change patterns then?"

"They shouldn't. A change means a ripple in time, caused by human hand."

I shook my head. The science made my temple somersault. If Mom and Dad hadn't hidden what they studied, maybe I would've learned enough to help Mekasha. "What's a ripple?"

He slid a globe across his desk. "It's a crack in the time layers."

My eyebrows popped up. "Time *layers?*"

"Yeah. People think time happens in a straight line, one minute after the other, year after year. Can't go back, can't go forward. But Jumpers know time is layered like sheets of paper wrapped around the earth. Each sheet is a year from the past, present, and future. Time in these layers happens at the same moment."

I held up my hand. "The 1980s are going on right now?" The pictures of Mom from then were hilarious. Big gold hoop earrings, feathered bangs.

"Yeah, right now. The layers are supposed to remain lined up, but . . ."

Mekasha paused and plucked a deck of cards from a drawer. He took a few off the top and fanned them out. "Imagine each of these five cards is a time layer." He pushed them together into one stack. "The layers line up, existing simultaneously. Then . . ."

He placed the stack on his desk and stabbed the center of it with a pair of scissors, making a hole.

"When a wormhole opens," he poked his thumb into the hole, "it causes a crack through the layers—a tunnel," he fanned the cards out about a quarter-inch, "and the layers no longer line up. They slip a smidge behind one another during their rotation with the earth."

I got it. "And that causes the stars to move a little each night from their normal positions. A rippled spot in the layers."

Mekasha zipped a finger across the cards. "Yeah. And at each end of the ripple is a wormhole that can be re-opened with enough tachyon energy."

"No wonder you map the stars." He'd searched years for Naya, and I'd selfishly hid Star from him.

He tapped his knuckles against an open trunk of rolled parchments. "Professor mapped, too. I've been drawing the star positions since the night Naya disappeared. Trying to figure out where her wormhole led to."

Professor stopped working on Galaxy and waved his hands from his chair, eyes wide. "You kept up my work, boy?"

"I did." Mekasha straightened, a big smile aimed at his mentor. "Ya taught me good."

"Are you close to knowing where Naya is?" I said.

"No." He plopped a thick stack of star maps onto the desk. "Not sure what to do with all these pictures." He moved to the sidewall, hovered his finger over a hanging United States map, then dabbed it atop New York City. "What I do know is tomorrow a wormhole opens here."

My heart skittered for him. "Of course, my parents' wormhole."

"When ya arrived ahead of yer parents, it was a gift, telling me the exact day and time a wormhole would open. I no longer need to come up with a big tachyon source to open a wormhole. Just a small vessel to keep it stable."

"Will we be able to see the hole?"

"Yeah. The wormhole creates a shimmer in the air. Like the one I followed the day ya arrived."

I gasped at the mention of the shimmery air. Is that what I saw in the Statue of Liberty before Aunt Maria went over the edge? No, it couldn't have been. The only tachyon sources we had were the butterflies, and Professor said they weren't strong enough to open a wormhole.

"Issy, ya all good?"

My eyes snapped up. "Uh, yeah, I'm fine." I shook off my imagination. The blur inside the statue must've been from my tears.

Professor shouted in triumph and raised Galaxy in his palm. "Here you go, daughter. Better now?"

Galaxy stretched her legs, one by one. Her wings jerked until they waved, smooth. Luna and Star flitted to Professor's arm to reunite with their sister. He waltzed around the room with his three daughters, whistling a tune in time with his steps. Mekasha joined them, his laughter bouncing around the boxcar like a ball.

Professor's face glowed at his family. I should have been happy for them, but my mind was too preoccupied. Flashes kept replaying of the moment Aunt Maria went over the side. And every repeat was an alternate outcome depending on what I could have done. Charged the dog. Grabbed Aunt Maria's legs. Anything to have saved her.

I stumbled to the couch with a strangled sob. "My sweet Aunt Maria."

Mekasha and Professor stopped their arms in mid-air and hurried over to me.

"Oh, Issy. Cry. Let it out." Professor hugged me to his side. "Your aunt was a remarkable woman."

The fear bottled inside since arriving in 1886 New York burst out from me. Why was it me to save my parents? Why did I have to get us out of *their* mess? And now, Aunt Maria was gone because I failed. I wanted to curl up with my laptop and write a new story, a happy one.

Mekasha patted my arm. "Not yer fault, Issy." He sounded so sure, so honest. "Maria acted out of love for ya."

I nodded as his warm smile inched into my spirit and edged out the pain.

"Mekasha, I, I'm sorry I hid Star from you." I stopped, too embarrassed to look at him.

"It's okay. I understand." He sighed. "I would've done the same for Naya."

A comfortable warmth spread over my face. Mekasha was the best thing to ever happen to me. If nothing else, at least we had a moment in time together. I gave him a quick side hug. "Where will you search for Naya?"

He shrugged. "I'm running out of time to find her location before yer wormhole opens."

I got up and went over to the United States map. "Where did all these datelines come from?" I traced my finger through

Dallas in Texas labeled with a date from years ago.

Professor joined me. He thumbed his nose. "I haven't seen this map for ages. Belonged to Bucky, a Time Jumper from around here. He tracked where the wormholes in New York City lead—the states they open to. I did the same after he passed the map to me."

"That's what it's for?" Mekasha examined the map, clicking his tongue. "I found it rolled up with yer things. Hung it for decoration."

I pointed to several dated lines crisscrossing the states. "Each line connects from New York to a spot in a different state. The dates must be the year the wormhole leads to, so—"

He cut me off, his gap-tooth grin breaking wide open. "Naya traveled to one of these spots."

"Yes," Professor said. "A wormhole can re-open in the same place. She must've voyaged to a location tracked on the map."

"But how do we decide where?" Mekasha fiddled with his pocket watches as if they were hot potatoes. His frustration urged me on.

I stared at the map. Dates, lines, dates, lines. Mekasha had said a ripple would crack the time layers when a wormhole opened. Constellations get out of sync with each layer. I riffled the transparent sheets of Mekasha's star maps like an old-time cartoon flipbook. The spread of stars came in and out of focus.

"Layer the star maps!" I blurted out.

Mekasha blew out his cheeks then released the air. "Wait, what?"

I pulled the star map dated the night Naya got caught by the wormhole. "This is when the wormhole opened for your sister."

I tacked the picture over New York. "The time ripple started here in New York City." The hand-drawn stars ran along the east coast, beginning in New York City and ending in Florida.

"Of course. Good job, Issy." Professor grabbed the other sheets and sifted through the pages. "Let's see. Place them in order, oldest on the bottom." He handed the pile to Mekasha. "Go on, boy. Place 'em up there."

Mekasha placed the stack of star maps over the U.S. map and stuck a pin in the top. My mind searched for patterns in the stars visible through each translucent sheet. The movement of the stars followed a path down the east side of the United States. But instead of the stars lining up between the pages, they blurred from the slipping of time layers. A ripple.

I moved in closer, and my eyes locked onto a spot where the stars returned to focus. "Here, the layers line back up." I pointed to a crisply defined star cluster. "New Bern, North Carolina, March 1893."

Mekasha slapped his knee. "Ya figured it out, Issy. My sister is in New Bern."

"Excellent!" Professor tipped his head at me.

I yawned. "Glad I could help."

"It's time ya got some rest," Mekasha said. "Tomorrow is a big day. We need to be ready for yer parents' wormhole."

"About the wormhole," I said. "How will you 'steer' yourself to New Bern 1893 if the path is between Arizona and here in 1886?"

Mekasha clicked his tongue and waggled his brow. "Another of my inventions." He pulled out a thick iron bracelet from a desk drawer. "This is a super magnetic metal." He slipped it onto his wrist and ran his finger over a tiny compass with a center lever, and then along ten yellow stones embedded down the band's middle. "The metal attracts and stores photons inside the stones while I travel through the wormhole. The energy and momentum of the photons create a gravitational pull to bend a spot in the wormhole just a little toward my destination."

"Woah!" I said. "You made this?" Gosh, Mekasha would be a great lab partner.

"Yep." He gazed at Professor, who intently stared back.

"Boy," Professor said with a scratch on his forehead. "This sounds familiar."

"Ya helped me. Do ya remember?"

Professor's eyes crossed then came into focus. "I-I do. But I didn't finish it, did I?"

"I finished it for both of us." Mekasha saluted and grinned.

"I'm proud of you, boy," Professor said.

More questions swirled in my mind. "How do you use the photons? And how do you know when you're at the right time and place? What kind of stones are those?" I paused to catch my breath.

Mekasha laughed. "Wish I would have shown ya this before. I'm glad ya are excited." He spun the bracelet. "Assuming my rate of speed through the wormhole remains steady, the bracelet will collect the same amount of photons during the time it takes to travel the length of one year. One quartz stone will light up for each year of stored photons."

The math flew through my head. "Seven lit stones means you're at 1893."

"Exactly! Ya got it." Mekasha smiled wide. "When the seventh stone lights up, then I push the compass lever in the direction of my jump. That releases the photons, and gravity will bend the wormhole toward where I want to go."

I chuckled in disbelief. "It's beyond an amazing invention." The science whirled my thoughts. "How many times have you used it?"

"Well . . ." Mekasha scrunched his nose. "This will be the first time. My other jumps were to random places."

A pit grew in my stomach. "Please don't get lost, Mekasha."

"I won't. Ya can't get rid of me that easy."

I turned and began taking down the star drawings. A faint pinhole in the U.S. map caught my eye. *Arizona.* The pinprick fell smackity-smack dab center of the state. "Professor, Arizona is marked. Is that the wormhole in my house, or is it a different one?" I leaned closer to see which city the pinhole was closest to, but Professor hastily untacked the map from the wall.

"Well, now," he said, "y-you could be correct." He folded the map and tucked it under his arm. "Or just that rascal traveler Bucky went to Phoenix. Or even just a pin to hold up the map. Now, time for bed, so scoot."

Sleepiness won out with the mention of bed, and my lion's yawn pulled my thoughts away from Professor's odd behavior over a simple pinprick. We settled in different spots—me in the loft bed, Professor on the couch, Mekasha in the armchair. I closed my eyes. The scene from my book played in my mind: Mom and Dad dragged away by soldiers. We had to get my parents before the soldiers did. No one could get in our way.

NEXT MORNING'S SUN heated the boxcar's metal walls. They creaked and popped from the warmth waking their old frames. I stretched from the bed and smoothed my shirt before slipping on my boots. Tonight was the night.

I put on my jacket and descended from the loft to find Mekasha had tidied the room, no doubt for when he brought Naya home. Professor stirred a pot of oatmeal over a small portable stove burner. The three sister butterflies flitted to my shoulders.

"Hello, girls." Their wings vibrated in response, giving my skin a tingle. I went to Professor. "Do you think they have enough tachyon energy to keep the wormhole open?"

Professor held the ladle mid-air and gazed at his daughters. "Star, yes. I'm not sure about Luna, and Galaxy needs more time to recover from Boss's attack."

Galaxy, the youngest daughter, flew up and bobbed in front of Professor's face. She turned in circles, clanking her wings at him. If she could pop Professor with a rivet, I imagined she'd aim for between his eyes. I laughed at her tweeness.

"She don't agree with ya. She wants to help." Mekasha strode over, his arm held out. Galaxy landed on him, and her sisters joined in a sign of unity.

Professor held up his hands, his eyes glistening. "Three against one. Everyone may come to the wormhole. We'll decide from there."

The three girls joined in the air and circled a figure eight above Professor as he blew kisses to them.

With that settled, we ate bowls of Professor's mush and hashed out the plan for my parents' arrival that night. Mekasha assured me we'd be in position ahead of the soldiers' arrival. After breakfast, we settled into various tasks. Professor made final checks on his daughters' wings, gears, and joints, all in top order. Mekasha tended over his *Tempus-Viator* in a pot on the little stove burner. He poured the potion into small glass vials and attached them to his jacket's chest pocket. The five little bottles clinked with his movements around the boxcar. He'd made extra for my parents and me.

I busied myself with packing my bag. The black corset was coming home for sure, plus the trinkets from the Bizarre Bazaar. I'd miss that place. I fit in there among the oddities. The vendors and visitors were refreshing, a place where creative people could just be themselves. And Gus from Cutter's Cut would make it into my edits. That way I'd level up the Bizarre Bazaar in *my* book to match their real world.

Rain pattered on the boxcar's metal top, and thunder drummed in the far distance. The weather mimicked the first page of my book when this adventure started. Not long now. My eyes watered at Mekasha. How would I ever find someone else like him? I didn't even want to.

"Hey ya, Issy." He deposited a marble jar onto his desk then joined me at the full-length mirror.

"Um, I—" My breath caught. I faced the glass, Mekasha at my side. Our reflections made my insides fuzzy: his tooth gap, me a head taller. What a pair we were.

"I will miss ya, too, Issy." He held my hand a moment, then

brought something out from behind his back. "I snatched it up from the catwalk."

"My mask. Thank you." I lifted it to my face for one last look. "I'll keep it to remind me of you, Professor, and the girls."

Professor heard his name and bounded over. Galaxy, Luna, and Star hovered around his head like a halo. He hugged me. "Issy, you never know when our paths will cross. I won't say goodbye, so I'll tell you to keep a wormhole warm for us." He winked.

"I'll miss you all," I whispered. My heart locked in a spot for each of them.

24 Secrets Revealed

THE SUN SUNK low and Mekasha announced it was time to leave for the docks. I was excited about being with Mom and Dad but scared about their reaction to Aunt Maria. The pain would be horrible. Mekasha gathered our bags, motioning Professor and me out the door.

"Goodbye, boxcar," I said to the cozy home with a great gadget workspace—Mekasha and Naya's home soon. I hoped.

Our hike to the docks took a bit longer with Professor in tow. But it gave Mekasha a chance to explain his plan. We'd jump through my parents' wormhole, me to Arizona and Mekasha to Naya's time, and he'd bring her back here. Professor agreed Mekasha could take Luna. Only after Luna clinked into a frenzy, convincing Professor she had enough energy for the roundtrip to New Bern. I'd take Star, and Galaxy would stay with Professor to gain strength.

We arrived at the docks after sunset. The waxing gibbous moon burned behind the clouds, and winds whipped the Statue of Liberty dedication banner against the steamship.

Mekasha led us to a worn wooden bench a short distance away. "Issy, let's see the picture in yer book to find whereabouts the wormhole opens."

My book was handy in the front pocket of my backpack. I flipped to page one. Mekasha held up the picture, eyeballing it with the nearby boat. "A match."

Professor leaned in. "Yes, the moon is in the same spot above the ship."

I placed my finger on the page. "My parents were here." I glanced to the right. "That's the direction the soldiers came from."

We scanned the docks. Light cracked the sky.

"We're close to the time," I said. Then, I cringed. "Are you sure the soldiers won't be here until later?" My stomach cramped at the idea of meeting those guys too soon. Then they'd drag us away before my parents ever got here, and all of this would be for nothing.

"Their headquarters are on the other side of the docks. At this hour, they'll be eating grub."

"Okay." He'd better be right. Once the soldiers heard the loud crack from the wormhole opening, it wouldn't be long before they headed over.

"Here. Issy, Mekasha." Professor handed Luna to Mekasha, Star, to me. He stifled a cry then retreated a couple of steps with Galaxy on his shoulder.

"Professor," Mekasha said, but the red-headed genius held

up his hand.

"I know you'll take care of her, boy."

Wind burst over the dock, full in our faces. Pain surged across my forehead. A shimmery wave rippled in the air before us. "Wormhole!" I steadied my feet for whatever was coming.

"Issy, come close," Mekasha called.

We huddled in front of the shimmer. Blue lightning struck the ground in front of the wormhole with a thunderous crash, throwing Mekasha and me backward.

A scream came from the swirling blue and purple mass.

I scrambled up to Mekasha's side. The wormhole stretched oblong, and my parents fell out.

"Luna, Star, go!" Mekasha instructed.

The automaton butterflies entered the wormhole and flitted around, using their tachyons to keep the cavity stable. The wind slowed, sending rain sprinkles across our faces.

I rushed to my parents and threw my arms around Dad's neck. "I found you, I found you," I sobbed into his chest.

He pulled back. "Issy? What, what happened?" His glazed eyes wandered to Mom. "Gina, did we?"

Mom squinted. "Hector, we were right—" She stiffened, her line of sight moving over my head. "Professor?"

I twisted around.

Professor wobbled, his eyes dazed. "Gina? Hector?"

They knew Professor?

Dad rushed to Professor's side with Mom following and tugging me along.

"Professor, yes, it's us." She embraced him with her free arm, keeping her other arm wrapped around my shoulder.

I peeked at Mekasha. His mouth hung in a silent, "Ah."

"*Mamá.*" I squirmed from her grasp. "How do you know Professor?"

She kissed the top of my head. "I love you so much, and we'll explain later." Her concentration swiveled over to Professor.

Later? After what I'd done for them? I gritted my teeth and scowled.

Mom looked at Professor. "We searched a long time for you."

"Yes, very long." Dad shook his head.

I raised my arms wide. "What do you mean you searched for him?"

A light clicked on in Professor's eyes. "How did you find me?"

"Oh, we've so much to tell you." Mom grasped his arm, unable to contain her joy.

"*Mamá,*" my voice cracked. "We don't have time." I pointed to Luna and Star, still flitting about the wormhole. "They won't last."

Her eyes snapped up. "*Sí, lo siento.* I didn't mean to get carried away." She pulled Professor near the wormhole. "Time to go."

Professor snatched back his arm. "No, I can't. I won't. I chose here as my home."

Mom's eyes flared. "You did this on purpose?"

"Gina, can you blame him?" Dad gathered her to his side. "He wanted to leave the time when he'd lost his girls."

"Wait. What?" Professor had left what time?

The rain picked up, and a shout carried through the air. "Stop!" The soldiers had arrived.

"We have to leave!" I elbowed Mekasha to go.

"No, you don't!" the voice barked.

I froze on the spot. Not the soldiers. It was Boss. Alone, her makeup streaked, hair a ratty mess. She scurried forward, about to swipe at Luna and Star, but Professor grabbed her before she got too close to the wormhole's opening, and they tumbled to the ground.

"Stop, you old fool!" she screamed. "I need the tachyons. It's the only way."

Professor cradled Boss tight in his arms. "What have you done to yourself? To your hearing? Lilian, no more."

What the atom? Lilian, his wife? I whipped my head around at the scene, the people. What changed? Had I already gone through the wormhole? Ended up in a time when Professor was with his wife? But *nada* had changed.

I clenched my fists and yelled, "What—is—happening?"

Mekasha, my anchor, came back to my side. He didn't say a word. He was just there.

Boss's shoulders shuddered. She let out an anguished cry to Professor, "I need to reset the timeline!"

Professor rocked her. "It won't bring back the girls. Not the way they used to be." Galaxy walked along Professor's arm to Boss's hand. The littlest *mariposa* raised her front legs and twirled like a ballerina. "You were a wonderful mother to our babies, Lilian."

Boss lifted her palm, her jaw slackened. She gasped, "Galaxy? My baby girl?" Her eyes whipped to Professor. "You did this?"

My mind unhinged. Mom and Dad knew Professor. Boss was Lilian—the mother of Luna, Star, and Galaxy. "What is going on, Professor?" I said.

His head rose, shaking. "Well, I. Lilian was my wife."

"Wife?" Heat seeped from my pores for Aunt Maria—Professor had shown nothing but puppy-dog love for her. I threw eye darts at him.

He released Boss. "Issy, wait. Lilian is my *ex*-wife."

"Ya claimed ya couldn't find yer wife," Mekasha said, his voice low and measured.

Professor wrung his hands. "I couldn't find her because my wife *Lilian* is gone, replaced by this, this Boss person." He spat out the name and glared at her. "Don't think I've forgotten what you did to Maria."

Dad held up his hand. "Wait, Maria, my sister? Issy, what happened?"

"*Papá*, I—"

Gunfire cracked from afar, sparking from the soldiers' guns who marched toward us. Their period uniforms were exactly like what I'd seen on the page of my book the night they took my parents.

"Go!" I guided Mom and Dad to the wormhole's opening. Mekasha followed, and we waved goodbye to Professor and Galaxy over our shoulders. "Run, Professor!"

I glanced at Boss, a heap on the ground. She'd experienced too much heartbreak. Maybe I could help her in a small way. Warn her.

"Boss, Sal is Skull!" I called to her.

In that nanosecond, she understood. Her eyes lit, and she gave me the slightest nod.

Mekasha pushed three vials of *Tempus-Viator* into my palm. "Good luck, Issy, my best friend. See ya again soon."

Jitters rocked through my chest as his image seared into my

head—a wink, a gap-toothed grin—then he jumped into the wormhole and sped off with Luna, his top hat bobbing from sight.

Star pulled me in with Mom and Dad, then made a dazzling spin with a shower of sparks, taking us down the tunnel toward home.

25 TRUTH

MY EYES FLUTTERED open to my family room, a hard pulse running through my noggin. I rubbed my temples. Total tamales, I was home, and no Whiz above the house. All was in balance, at peace. I steadied myself against the couch and spotted Mom and Dad sprawled on the floor near the fireplace.

"*Mamá, Papá!*" I hurried to them, nudging their shoulders.

Mom moaned, coming around first, then Dad. I gave them a moment to deal with the pain brought on by time jumps, but they gathered themselves up to the couch without even tripping.

"How do you feel?" I watched their faces for signs of brain scramble. Their alert eyes remained on me.

Dad took my hand. "*Bueno,* Issy. Fine. I'm so happy we're all home."

"Wait, you don't have a headache? Stomach pain?" Maybe their prior jumps had helped to reduce the effect?

"No, no, I'm good." Dad glanced at Mom.

"*Sí*, me, too." She folded her hands in her lap and nodded at me. "*Querida,* we have a lot to tell you."

I plopped onto the floor, wide-eyed, hoping for no more lies. Maybe the hole in my heart from them leaving me out of everything would fill in and puff up like warm *pan dulce*.

Dad coughed and pushed his glasses up his nose. "We, ah, haven't been studying weather patterns here in Arizona. We won't bore you with the details, but we worked with Professor long ago in New York."

My spine jolted upright. "Professor in our time?"

"*Sí*. Marcus Stanley Mitchell," Mom said in awe. "A brilliant scientist."

I translated Professor's name into initials. *MSM*. Where had I seen those letters? Mom glitched my thinking process with her continued tribute to Professor.

"He was at the forefront of time travel. We were on the verge of locating static wormholes, ones leading to specific times and places. Not random years and locations."

Dad chimed in. "But then Professor lost his daughters in a car accident in our time."

That explained why Professor had referred to Liberty Island instead of Bedloe's Island. He'd recalled the place in my time when his daughters died.

"Too much for him." Mom exhaled. "His wife, Lilian, also an exceptional scientist, fell into deep misery. Then she left."

I scooched closer to Mom and leaned against her legs. Boss was a despicable person, and I blamed her for Aunt Maria, but I imagined she'd turned from Lilian to Boss to escape the agony.

I understood hiding behind characters.

"We continued time travel experiments with Professor," Dad said. "But his heart wasn't in it anymore, and he disappeared."

"A horrible loss." Mom frowned. "What happened to them broke us. We buried ourselves in experiments, trying to find Professor. We're his only *familia*."

That was why they never had time for me, because they'd been hunting in time for Professor. And why they didn't want me in their lab. Risk me uncovering the truth. I watched their faces. What other secrets? "When did you discover the wormhole in this house?"

"Several months ago." Dad leaned back into the cushions. "Star mapping helped us to locate it."

"Mapping the stars? Mekasha does that, too."

Dad laughed. "No doubt Professor taught him. We charted the stars with Professor as well. He'd found the maps in an old storage room in our New York lab and deciphered their purpose."

"Do you think the wormhole here in our family room is static?" I questioned Mom with my eyes. "It'll always lead between here and 1886 New York?"

"Well, it's what our hypothesis shows, at least." She pressed her palm to my cheek. "*Querida*, somehow your book connected to the wormhole as a channel to an *alternate* 1886 New York. We don't know how, but we'll figure it out. Together."

I leaned into her hand and smiled. But something didn't calculate for me. The alternate steampunk world came from my imagination, right? How could a wormhole lead to a made-up world?

Mom continued. "A couple of days after moving in, we

found two mechanical butterflies on the coffee table."

"Luna and Galaxy." Tingles rolled along my legs.

"*Sí,*" Dad said. "The butterflies perplexed us, but when they animated and showed intelligence, we knew they were Professor's work. He must've gotten them to us across the static wormhole. We found the thumb drive of his valuable data and hid it in the barn lab."

My eyes fell. "All about Professor's research."

Mom settled to her knees beside me. "Isadora, *lo siento.* You're right. We got caught up with Professor. His work fascinated us." She took my hands into hers. "But Professor does not want to return. No more wormholes, no more time travel."

"But I won't see Mekasha." Numbness spread through my limbs. I'd never see him again.

We sat silent for a few minutes, Mom at my side. What I always wanted—my parents' attention. But misery burned, something I hadn't felt before. Because I'd never lost a *true* friend.

I pled my case to Mom about seeing Mekasha, but I was stopped by a key jiggling the front door lock. We all stood at the interruption. The knob turned, and a ball of energy came in.

"*La familia!*"

"Aunt Maria!" I screamed, barreling into her chest with a hug. My toes melted into the ground, and I blubbered like a Chunk. "My wonderful *tía.*" The guilt of failure slid off my shoulders like a loose shawl.

"*Mija,* you're back." She swooped me up with one arm and spun me around, setting me down to eyeball me head to toe. Her other arm, the one Fred had bitten, was cast in bright pink and held in a sling.

"*I'm* back? What about you?" Jitters pushed aside my grief as if a thousand metal butterflies scurried over my skin. "How? I saw you fall."

"She fell?" Dad rushed to her and checked her arm. "*Hermana*, are you okay?"

"*Sí, estoy bien.* My arm will heal." Aunt Maria bustled to the couch. Dad sat next to her while Mom and I sat on the floor, snuggled up to one another.

As Aunt Maria got settled in and Dad fussed over her, I handed out the three vials of Mekasha's *Tempus-Viator*, skipping myself. I could handle two jumps. But Dad insisted I have one. I took back his vial and gulped it, biting my lips at the tangy flavor.

"How'd you survive the fall?" I stared at Aunt Maria.

She fanned herself. "*Oye*, miraculous, *mija*. The wormhole was all warm and fuzzy."

"You fell into a wormhole?" I searched my parents' tense faces for answers. "How'd a wormhole open inside the Statue of Liberty? The butterflies didn't have enough tachyon energy to do that." A nod passed between them.

"*No sé*, but I landed here." Aunt Maria's words spilled like a tipped glass of milk before my parents could answer. "You weren't back yet, though. But today. Today, you did it." Her tears fell. She rubbed the cat's eye marble of her necklace between her fingers. "You got your *Papá* and *Mamá* home. *You* did, *mija*."

More questions for Mom and Dad twirled about my mind. I turned to them. "Without tachyons, how'd the wormhole remain stable for Aunt Maria to travel?" It didn't make sense. The butterflies couldn't have opened the wormhole, Aunt Maria didn't have tachyons to keep it secure, and my parents hadn't any on their trip either. "Why didn't your wormhole collapse when you first got sucked in? Mekasha said you must've had a tachyon vessel on you."

Mom held out her cat's eye marble on her necklace. She pointed to Aunt Maria's matching charm. "These are vessels, although weak ones. Good for one jump. We had very few tachyons to make these."

My lips trembled. "But you didn't make one for me?"

Aunt Maria's excitement barreled through my voice. "I've had a vessel on me the whole time?" She gasped, eyeing my Dad. "*Hermano,* you're sneaky."

"You got me." He shrugged at her, avoiding my question. "I had to make sure you'd be safe, Maria, if something like this happened."

She kissed the marble, and then her tone turned thoughtful. "How are Mekasha, the girls?" She blushed. "And Professor? If only he and I met in this time."

"They're all fine." I left out the part about Lilian, aka Boss. Aunt Maria and Professor had connected so easily, I didn't want to hurt my *tiá*. "Mekasha found his sister's location, and Luna took him there. Professor and Galaxy are together."

"I am so happy for them," she said. "*¿Dónde está* Star?"

"Wait, how could I forget?" My heart thundered. "Where's Star?"

A clickity-clack came from behind the armchair. Star rose, slow and choppy. I held out my palm, and she landed with a thud then crawled up my arm. Her tachyon energy zinged over my skin. "Hey, Star. You look okay." I stroked her wing and caught Mom's eyes. "I want to visit Mekasha."

Her face startled. "No, Isadora. You can't."

"Why? You said the wormhole is static. It opened between here in the family room and 1886 New York City: Professor's tent, at the Statue of Liberty, at the docks. Always when I—"

Blood rushed to my head, and my body numbed. A wormhole formed in all those places. When I was around. I was the one who got sick, got the headaches. No one else.

"Issy." Dad's voice wobbled with caution. "Time travel is worse on your body than on ours."

The neurons in my brain fired off and connected the facts. Time travel was worse for me because . . .

"I'm a tachyon source," I whispered. Whiz hadn't opened the wormhole in my family room after all. It was me.

Dad drew a sharp breath. "*Sí*. We suspect that tachyons infused with your DNA."

My heart rocketed. "How is that even possible?"

"*Mamá* and I time jumped long ago. We were lucky to have found our way back."

"*Sí*," Mom said. "I was pregnant with you during our jump. We hypothesized that the tachyon force merged with your genetic makeup while your cells developed. We told no one. Not even Aunt Maria or Professor. It's a secret we've carried for years. We didn't want you to become anyone's science experiment."

Star nestled closer to my neck, and her energy hummed through me. Of course! She knew I was a vessel. All the girls must've sensed my energy. Even Sal/Skull's little box triggered around me. That's why he followed me at the bazaar and why his new tachyon detector picked up a strong signal at the Statue of Liberty. It was me. Funny, though, how the detector stopped working when it was close to me. I clicked my number rings, thinking back to each time. The detector malfunctioned when I held out my hand!

"Titanium." I stared at my parents. "It blocks tachyon detection, doesn't it." Like the cloth Professor gave me to wrap Galaxy.

Dad smiled. "Yes, a discovery made by Professor. I made your number rings. Not near enough titanium to fully shield you but enough to fool a tachyon detector. We didn't want anyone figuring out that you're a vessel."

I stood and paced; my thoughts went sideways. Star held fast to my shoulder. Could there be long-term damage from being a vessel? Would my body be destroyed after the tachyon energy ran out? I faced my parents. "How long have you known?"

"Since you were little," Dad said. "We often saw glimmer spots in the air around you." He waved his fingers. "Small ones, not big enough to open a wormhole, but we weren't sure how fast your ability would grow. The frequency of the glimmers increased these past few months."

Childhood memories stormed my head: twinges of pain behind my eyes, blurry vision, sparkly lights, upset tummy. My child's brain thought the shimmery air was from my imaginary superpowers. The doctor said it was migraines, but it was really because I was a vessel. "No wonder I got sick after the time jumps." I returned to the floor near Mom. "Because some of the tachyons were taken from me?"

She put her arm around my shoulders. "*Sí*. You can't open any more wormholes. Do you understand? It's dangerous to your body."

"That's why we moved here," Dad said. "There's too much data and too many variables for us to compute on our own. We needed the wormhole so we could find Professor, hoping he knew of a way to remove the tachyons from your DNA."

No, I didn't want to lose my tachyons, did I? I wouldn't have the chance to tell Professor and Mekasha I was a vessel. Professor would be giddy to find out I was like his daughters.

Hmm, his daughters. Why had Professor time jumped to leave Luna and Galaxy with Mom and Dad in the first place? For some reason, he believed we needed tachyons.

The date patterns from Professor's star maps flipped around my head. Oh, oh, the pinpoint in Arizona state. Marvelous molecules! "He reset the timeline."

"*¿Qué?* Who did what?" Mom said.

I giggled, bubbling into laughter. "Brilliant."

"Issy, what is it?" Dad tilted his head at me.

Woo-wee, I'd figured it out before them. "This wasn't the first time you found Professor in 1886."

"It wasn't?" Mom wrinkled her forehead at Dad.

He pushed up his glasses, and his eyes lit. "*Sí*, of course! Go ahead, Issy, explain it."

I smiled at his confidence in me. "We've done this trip before. Professor had already experienced the three of us coming through. That's why I found Arizona marked on his map. My theory is we ended up stuck in 1886 the first time, captured by the soldiers because my tachyon strength wasn't yet strong enough to re-open the hole at the docks and get us all home. I had only enough energy to open it here in the house and keep it stable for one trip. By our second jump, my energy was stronger.

That's why the hole remained open in the family room for Aunt Maria to use."

"*Sí.* And I had Galaxy to take me through." Aunt Maria tapped her forehead, sending her bracelets jangling. "*Bueno,* I'm catching on."

"*Esperar,* wait, wait." Mom waggled her hands above her head.

"*Mamá,* Professor reset the timeline," I explained again. "Mekasha said the original memories can disappear for the jumpers if a timeline is reset. That's why we don't remember."

Dad whistled low. "It's more than our research ever uncovered."

"*Sí, Papá.* Professor couldn't stop what would happen. So, he traveled here *before* the wormhole took you, and he planted Luna and Galaxy to help us. He didn't know I was a vessel."

"*Oye,* my Professor," Aunt Maria swooned.

"No wonder he knew my name when I met him at his tent." I chuckled. Professor Marcus Stanley Mitchell, you're a magnificent man. His name floated before my eyes, the initials: *MSM.* Mr. Automaton at City Hall! That was why he'd had a familiar personality.

The evidence of Professor's plan rushed my brain, sending my synapses into electrical overdrive. Gus at Cutter's Cut had met me before. Steampunk 1886 New York wasn't created through my book; it always existed somewhere in history—I wrote my novel based on past experiences there. I hadn't made it up. The memories must've been buried in my subconscious, not erased by the time reset. Was that because my tachyon power was so strong?

Oh, *mighty skyscraper!* Is Jocko Jones real? Could I find him if I went back?

Dad waved his hand at me. "Earth to Issy. I know this is a lot to take in. What I don't understand is why Professor didn't warn us when he time jumped here. We could've prevented all this."

Professor's daughters' car accident raced to mind. "Because, Professor had said, 'Terrible things happen when you interfere too much, tell people of things that will happen to them. Fate is fate.'" His eerie expression made me shiver that day. "Professor couldn't put us in danger by making a huge change or telling us the future. He could only reset the timeline and plant the extra tachyon vessels to give us a better chance."

Tears wet Mom's eyes. "Professor risked brain scramble, even his butterfly girls, to save us."

I couldn't believe the lengths Professor had taken. "And it wasn't just the butterflies he left for us. I have a feeling he put his DNA into the automaton robot in City Hall just in case we needed help. He must have known we'd end up back in that time again."

Mom raised her brows. "I bet he put his DNA into more than just the robot—who knows how many *Professors* he planted back in that time, waiting to help save us?"

"Humph." Aunt Maria heaved herself off the couch, settling on the floor near me. "You saved us, *mija*." She patted my cheek. "You are strong and smart. I'm proud of you."

I hugged her, knowing I was more than the friendless science geek I'd let define me. I was a niece, a daughter, a true friend.

A twinge tugged at me. Mekasha. He accepted me, my mistakes, all the way to the end. I hoped he was with Naya, but something bothered me. If Mom and Dad were right about the wormhole being static between here and alternate 1886 New York, then did Mekasha's magnetic photon bracelet really work to bend the wormhole toward his sister's location? Or, did he land here? I craned my neck, looking around the room.

"Isadora, listen." Mom whacked through my thoughts like a bat to a *piñata*. She pulled my hands into hers and smiled. "We promise to make time for you."

I nodded and squeezed her hands, knowing I could trust her word.

And now I understood all the things that made me different, and that was okay. I looked forward to starting school here in Cornville and enjoying our new home at 77 Yucca Road. It was not just because it kept me close to Mekasha, Professor, and the girls, at least in my heart, but I was ready to find my tribe. Friends I could count on. All I needed was to be myself.

I smiled at Aunt Maria and reached for Mom and Dad's hands, excited to join them in their lab, to share in their type of science and them in mine. I'd leave the time-jumping adventures for my next book . . . *maybe.*

Dani Camarena feels most at home nestled within the trees and shadows of the forest. There, her imagination soars, dreaming up fantastical quests and lovable characters. When not writing, Dani can be found having adventures with her sons, snowboarding, or camping in the mountains. She lives in Idaho with her husband, boys, dogs, cats, rabbits, and maybe one day a llama. Check out what Dani is up to at:
www.danicamarena.com

Patricia Dewitt-Grush and **Robin Dewitt** are identical twin artists and art teachers specializing in Fine Art, Illustration, and Graphic Design. They both graduated from the Maryland Institute College of Art with degrees in Illustration—Robin graduating with a master's in Digital Design. Both artists have an extensive array of work experience, illustrating for publishers such as Stemmer House, Charlesbridge, Scholastic, Time Life, and many more.

www.DewittStudios.org

Want more insightful, empowering, fun children's books?
Want activities and links to go along with the story?
Visit us at lawleypublishing.com

For updates and info on New Releases follow us at

lawleypublishing

@kidsbookswithheart

LAWLEY PUBLISHING

Printed in the USA
CPSIA information can be obtained
at www.ICGtesting.com
LVHW020058210624
783564LV00014B/1039